If the Shoe Fits

If
the Shoe
Fits

There's a Man to Match

Nic Clark

*In loving memory of the original Shoe Queen, 'D',
the best mother-in-law a girl could wish for.*

Prologue

"So, just how many husbands have you had, then?" asked the hairdresser.

Luckily, she wasn't drinking coffee at the time. When I said, "Well, technically, three," she would have certainly choked or spat it out.

"Wow, Hannah!"

You may think I'm crazy but just bear with me for a few minutes. I have a theory that the shoes we love somehow tie into the type of men we pick and that we choose a mate according to our taste in shoes. Yep, I know it sounds bizarre but let me try to explain where I'm coming from.

You're in a long-term relationship with a great guy but somehow the relationship has lost its spark along the way. He is a good man, but you take each other for granted, and you've been with him so long you can't remember why you fell for him in the first place. You love him but you're not in love with him; maybe you're still together because that's the way it has always been.

Let's picture the relationship in footwear terms. Is your partner/husband like an old pair of slippers? You've had them for years (as you have him), they're not stylish or sexy, you wouldn't even be seen in them in public, they have holes in, they're tatty and should really go in the bin. They probably smell a bit too, but somehow you just can't part with them.

You've been through so much together, you and the slippers. Your mum bought them for you when you had that nasty bout of flu (about a hundred years ago) to cheer you up when you had to miss the office Christmas party. You were wearing them the night your sister went into labour – you were so excited, you rushed to the maternity unit still wearing them and that gorgeous doctor was laughing at them, and your embarrassment! You go way back, you and the slippers, but let's be honest here – maybe even brutal – those slippers are not fit for purpose anymore, just like your relationship.

On the other hand, they are sooo comfortable, you can't imagine wearing any others. When you have a terrible day at work, you get home, put them on and just feel that all is well with the world. They feel warm and comforting, like after those terrible nightmares when you were little, and your dad cuddled you until you fell back to sleep.

Your relationship with your man is similar. You don't really talk anymore, he probably wouldn't notice if you dyed your hair blue, but he's always there, in the background, a comforting presence.

So, this is my story of shoes and men, my experiences with one or two of them and some others I've met along the way. I hope you enjoy it and maybe some of the characters will ring a bell with you.

Part One

Trying On for Size

Lesson: Never Buy a Pair of Shoes Without Trying Them On

Most girls (and some boys!) love shoes. We know what we like, and we go for it. Let's be honest, we've all done it: seen the most fabulous pair of shoes (far too expensive for our meagre budget), tried them on, fallen in love and bingo! We feel a million dollars in them, our friends are green with envy, and the shoes have pride of place in the wardrobe. Sometimes we love them so much we have them in every available colour (or is that just me?)!

We put them on and instantly feel good, like a great haircut, but the shoes last longer. I have shoes that have been with me for years, no longer remotely fashionable, perhaps a little scuffed, but I still love them and couldn't bear to say goodbye to them. Nothing beats feeling good – apart from eating chocolate, obviously – and I believe shoes are a real pick-me-up.

If there are any fellas reading this, most of you will never understand; perhaps it's a girl thing. I guess it's on a level with 'you can never watch too many football matches'. So, you go back to the Liverpool game, and we'll go shoe and man shopping.

One subtle difference between shoes and men: if you've made a mistake with the shoes, at least you can take them back to the shop for a refund, unless you've worn them, in which case you can give them to a friend or put them in a plastic bag and donate them to a charity shop. If only we could do that with men, wouldn't life be simple?

Unfortunately, we pick a man that is not right for us, he looked fabulous initially, but we then realise that, like the shoes we did not try on first, he's a bit tight, not quite how he looked in the picture and doesn't fit comfortably at all.

I have a theory that the shoes we love correspond to the type of man we need in our lives. It's a question of trying before you buy, seeing if your friends like them, but not too much or they'll want the same ones, and trying lots on until you find what works for you, which is the fun bit. It worked for me, although I admit to getting through some very unusual footwear over the years until I found the perfect fit; I'll reveal all later!

See if you agree and have fun!

In the Beginning

I grew up in a small town on the south coast. That's my first untruth, as I'm not sure I've come close to growing up yet, although I'm quite close in age to God's grandmother, but I'm working on that. Anyhow, one of my earliest memories is The Red Shoes.

Being the youngest of three children, my mother had got the hang of parenting by the time I made an appearance, so it was difficult to pull the wool over her eyes or try anything that hadn't been done by the others. I had fun trying but rarely got away with it. She was strict, manners were very important, as was being 'seen and not heard', which basically I failed at every available opportunity.

My mother was old school. Shoes were always practical, serviceable and sensible. And boring. Three pairs were adequate: one for school, one for playing out in and a pair for best. Best what? I never did get a straight answer, just a clip round the ear for my cheek.

I had to wear the best shoes on Sunday if my nan was coming for tea, or if we went to visit one of the aunts, of which there were quite a few, some I loved, some I wasn't so keen on. One of them, Auntie Hett, always looked so glamorous in her gorgeous brightly coloured high heels that I decided, aged about eight, she was my favourite person, and I wanted to be just like her when I grew up. I had no idea back then she was the black sheep of the family and had caused no end of grief, leaving her husband for a man half her age and causing Nan to almost have a heart attack. I adored her, still do, even though she's over eighty by a fair way (she'd kill me if I told you her age) and she now wears more age-appropriate footwear.

So, my shoes were brown or black but always hideous. On the plus side, I didn't suffer the indignity of having to wear my older sisters' leftovers. She has very narrow feet and mine are wider. Also, shoe buying was quite an event. Feet must be measured by a trained sales assistant and bought to last. This event occurred every three months, unless I complained my shoes were pinching, in which case the expedition was brought forward accordingly.

I got wise and frequently complained my shoes hurt if they were particularly hideous, but unfortunately Mother was always one step ahead (sorry for the pun), so the next pair would be even uglier. I remember throwing one of my nastiest shoes out of the window of the bus on the way home from school thinking she would have to buy me some new ones if I said I'd lost it. Wrong again! On that occasion, she actually made me go to school in my sisters' old ones and boy they really did hurt. A week and some nasty blisters later, an identical pair to the ones I'd thrown out of the bus window were purchased. Lesson learned; I was never going to outsmart my mother. It was at this point I learned how fragile friendships could be. What possessed

Rebecca Anderson to tell her mother what I'd done on the school bus when our mothers were friends?

So, it seemed I was destined to have to wear the ugliest shoes in the world for my entire childhood and life was about as bad as it could get when… ta-da! The Red Shoes came to live with me.

Strangely, I don't remember the actual purchase of The Red Shoes. It may have been a birthday treat, but I do clearly remember going to sleep every night with The Red Shoes on my bedside table, still in the box with the lid off, so they'd be the first thing I saw when I awoke the next morning.

And so, the story, and my shoe obsession, begins.

★★★★★

If you look up 'shoe' on Wikipedia, you read the following:

> "A shoe is an item of footwear intended to protect and comfort the human foot. Though the human foot can adapt to varied terrains, it is vulnerable, and shoes provide protection."

My view of shoes is more along the lines of a supportive role: they can complete an outfit and can make you feel special. We adapt to the varied terrains in our lives by wearing the appropriate footwear, and the man we choose can detract from or enhance our lives in a similar way. For example, we wouldn't wear our Jimmy Choos to go hiking, would we? In my humble opinion, your shoes will complement you, and your partner should do the same.

Not all women feel the need for protection by a man; we're not in the twentieth century anymore. We are independent creatures. Let me tell you about some of my shoes, how comfortable – or otherwise – they turned out to be, which ones I kept, and which ones turned out to be totally unsuitable.

I told you about The Red Shoes in the beginning, which, over the years, were replaced by more red shoes. What can I say? I love red shoes. But, as you will discover, they haven't always loved me back.

Anthony

This is Anthony. He likes it pronounced 'Anth-ony' as opposed to 'Ant-ony'. This may lead you to suspect he has a slight lisp, which he does. Please do not call him Tony, ever, or – even worse – Ant. He will tell you he's not an insect.

Anthony is the pair of shoes that tend to get left in the back of the wardrobe. They're plain and sensible in a rather dreary shade of beige (is there any other type of beige?). The type of shoes that make you question why and when you would have ever bought them; possibly for a job interview when it was imperative to dress like a responsible adult, or maybe your nan gave them to you.

He is quite traditional, almost old-fashioned really, but that can have its advantages, as you will see later. He is not (in my opinion) particularly attractive but not unpleasant to look at. He's practical, versatile and quite thoughtful, often wondering why he's overlooked in favour of someone else.

Best described as ordinary, nothing about Anthony stands out from the crowd. He's reliable, always there if you need him and doesn't need your attention all the time. He's quite happy with his own company, which works for me, as he's not the most fascinating man in the world. Not boring exactly, but just too ordinary for me.

He attended the local comprehensive school, which he feels a little embarrassed about. He can be snobby about people's backgrounds. Although far from stupid, his grades were average (surprise surprise!) and university was never an option due to that and family finances.

Some family background for you: his parents have been married since their early twenties and have a daughter Moira, four years older than Anthony. Moira lives and works in Japan, unmarried but in love with her married boss, not that she'd ever admit it.

His father Bill was an engineer until taking early retirement due to ill health and his mother worked part time as a school canteen assistant. All very ordinary.

Anthony is the kind of man that works in insurance and isn't overly ambitious. I'd call him a bit of a plodder. He never gets overly excited about anything, never gets higher than a three on the angry scale, just gets a bit agitated at times. Very 'middle of the road', I'd call him.

On the plus side, he's reliable, would never let you down and is always courteous. He will open doors for you and makes sure you're under the umbrella in the rain, even if he gets wet. For goodness' sake, don't try and split the bill in the restaurant, he'd be mortified!

He has had a few girlfriends, none lasting more than a few months, partly due to his mother's disapproval and partly natural causes. Anthony could be viewed as picky where potential girlfriends are concerned. He'd disagree, of course; he just feels women of today can be a little too forward and don't really understand how to look after a man properly. Hmmm, wonder where he got that opinion from. He's also a bit unsure about sex. Mother, of course, brought him up with the view that nice girls don't before marriage, very old-fashioned in my opinion (especially when she was three months' pregnant with Moira when she married Bill). So, the women he's had sex with are clearly not marriage material, and those who haven't are probably frigid! Poor Anthony and his views from the 1950s.

A good timekeeper, polite and well mannered, he likes things done properly. Shoes always polished, nails trimmed and clean but never manicured, good grief, he thinks only gay men have a manicure! In fact, there's nothing bad about Anthony, if you want a man who still lives at home with his mum aged thirty-something! He does do his own ironing, though; his mother just can't get the collars how he likes them.

Anthony can't abide disorganisation on any level, or tardiness for any reason. A place for everything and everything in its place is just one of his mantras. He's the sort of man who, arriving at your home, will immediately remove his shoes, placing them tidily on the mat and will rearrange other people's shoes that are not paired properly. He does have potential, but I think would be a bit hard work, to be honest.

I said earlier he's versatile: like the shoes I've named after him, you could dress him up or down accordingly. He will fit in with your work colleagues, never embarrassing you at the office Christmas party. In fact, your boss won't even remember his name by tomorrow.

Your friends will think he's okay, they may even like him, and there's no danger of him running off with your best friend, it wouldn't enter his head. Anyway, he doesn't run anywhere, it's not dignified.

Another potential plus, he's not a sports fan, either as a spectator or a participant. Having said that, he can be a little judgemental, maybe even opinionated. He'll happily tell you he's not keen on macho rugger types, loud-mouthed football fans or hobbyists who he finds very boring. In fact, anyone who has an interest in anything other than work he may consider a little obsessed.

So, if you're not enthralled by the prospect of rainy Saturdays on the touchline at football, followed by a three-hour post-mortem in the pub with the lads, he may be your ideal man.

He probably drives a Ford or similar, never anything that could be perceived as a bit flash. He dislikes loud people; anyone who draws attention to themselves would be regarded as an embarrassment of enormous proportions, positively vulgar, to quote his mother. Talking of her, he does call her Mother, as opposed to Mum.

If he's not for you at the moment, don't write him off completely, he'll be there if you need him. His mother may not approve of you, though, especially if your name is Chardonnay or Mercedes, she'd like him to marry Susan. You know the one, went to the same junior school as

Anthony, has never been drunk or dyed her hair, a 'nice girl', as Anthony's mother would say. In fact, Susan would be a perfect match, so if you're thinking Anthony is perfect for you then you'd better get in quick!

Anthony and me (I know! What was I thinking?)

Having recently been dumped – or, more accurately, forgotten about – by a man you'll meet later, I was feeling a little sorry for myself. So, when Anthony asked me if I'd like to go for a drink, I agreed. Looking back, my ego was on the floor, and I suppose I was flattered. Also, I'm never one to turn down a drink. There were red flags from the outset. Anthony suggested we meet outside The Old Castle pub, as he thought most of the bars in town were overcrowded, overpriced and full of young people and very loud music. The Old Castle is more of a traditional pub, full of elderly gentlemen drinking a pint of bitter and doing *The Times* crossword. In his defence, it was quiet, warm with a roaring open fire and very cosy. We had a couple of drinks, general chitchat and, although not unpleasant, the evening was nothing to write home about. I had had quite a long day at work and was not disappointed when Anthony suggested calling it a night (as he had promised his mother he would not be late home) and we arranged to meet the following week for dinner.

Over our dinner date at Carmelos, I told Anthony about the girls' night out I had had the previous Friday.

Second red flag: Anthony's facial expression when I told him we had been to a karaoke bar in fancy dress, as ABBA. We had, in fact, had an amazing fun-filled evening and a lot of laughs, but Anthony's reaction made me feel like a naughty schoolchild who should know better. In fact, all our dates turned out in a similar vein. The more horrified Anthony appeared at my behaviour, the more outrageous I became. My inner child seemed to be ever present during my short relationship with Anthony. Against his better judgement, and despite the blue streak in my hair, I was taken home to meet the parents after a couple of months. Unfortunately, I had neglected to mention the fact that I was having my nose pierced earlier that week, and although there was no verbal reaction, the expression on Anthony's mother's face told me all I needed to know about this lady and where Anthony got his views from.

On the way home, we had our first big argument, with Anthony asking why I had not seen fit to discuss it with him first. Admittedly, my response was a little childish. I asked him if he felt the need to discuss with me when he had a shave (in truth, it was a little more personal than that, but you don't need to hear what I really said). My point being, I can and will do what I like with my own body, and I certainly don't need to ask anyone else's permission. If I'm honest, I should have ended it there and then, but we drifted on for a few more weeks until just before my birthday when I informed him, purely because I was so excited, that I would be getting a tattoo on my shoulder. Had Anthony not been choking on his glass of Malbec, I think he would have had plenty to say about that. When he managed to regain his composure, he simply said, "I am assuming you are joking?" Although I like to think of myself as a bit of a comedian, I assured him that I was deadly serious, and it was something I had always wanted. At this point, we both realised we were totally unsuited, and we should part company. Ever the gentleman, Anthony insisted on driving me home and giving me the present he had already bought for my birthday. Unsurprisingly, it was two tickets to an opera that his boss had recommended. Don't judge me, but I'm sure you've worked out by now I'd sooner shave my legs with a blunt razor than go to the opera. I very kindly informed him that, while not ungrateful, I'm sure he would enjoy taking someone else.

On to pastures new.

Ben

Meet Ben. Don't let the long hair and ripped jeans deter you, he's not a surfer really, just dresses like he could be.

Ben is like your red Converse, a little frayed round the edges, a bit scruffy looking. The ones you've had for years but still love, even if they're falling to bits. Unlike our friend Anthony, who likes to use his full name, Ben is short for Benjamin and woe betide anyone who calls him anything other than Ben, except his nana, whom he adores and can do no wrong in Ben's eyes! (She often calls him Benny, but don't tell him I told you.) It's reciprocal, Ben has been Nana's favourite since he drew his first breath. She has had a colourful life and done things her children are embarrassed about, but she and Ben share the same zest for life and wacky sense of humour.

From a big family (three brothers and two sisters), there's not a selfish bone in his body. Everything was shared – toys, clothes, food – everything, that is, except Nana! She was and still is known as Ben's nana, much to the amusement of the siblings. No jealousy in this house, just good-natured teasing. Any potential girlfriends must pass muster with Nana, which isn't too difficult as she loves almost everyone. "Everyone has good in there somewhere, sometimes we just need to put on our varifocals to see it. I'm sure even Donald Trump has something nice about him, but it certainly is not his hairstyle!" is Nana's favourite line currently.

Ben has a sense of humour that borders on ridiculous. This man is fun loving and up for anything. The sillier the better. He once superglued his hands together to see how strong the glue really was, which would've been funny, but he was twenty-four at the time. It was probably Nana's idea, to be fair. His friends and family adore him, and he's never short of female attention due to his boyish grin and enthusiasm for everything.

Fun loving also means scatty, forgetful and occasionally irresponsible. Ben has a serious nut allergy but has no idea where his EpiPen is, which is needed for emergencies that could prove serious. He needs a girlfriend who can also be his mother/carer/appropriate adult. He will come over to your place and cook you an incredible meal, but your pots and pans will need to be replaced, as he will have burnt a few things on the first attempt. There won't be many coffee mugs left in your cupboard either. "Sorry, the handle just came off in my hand," is a regular thing. Obviously, the contents of the cup will have landed on your cream rug; this man is an accident looking for somewhere to happen. Lost keys are pretty much a daily occurrence. On one occasion, the police were called regarding 'a man on a conservatory roof, trying to break into a house through the open bathroom window'. This story ended with the police taking him to the A&E department, and a fracture that required a plastic boot for a while. He does spend a fair amount of time at the minor injury department; I expect he's got a seat reserved for him. Everything from the superglue incident to hitting himself on the head with a hammer – yes, really. My favourite story is the one where he climbed up the drainpipe to scare the kids on Halloween by tapping on the bedroom window and the drainpipe broke; no bones broken but I hear he had some impressive bruising and couldn't sit down for a week. He'll certainly keep you entertained but he may not be a great choice if you have a nervous disposition.

In many ways, Ben could be your perfect man: kind, funny, handsome, caring, but – there's always a but – he's so friendly he may forget you're his date when he sees an old friend in the pub and gets reminiscing about old times. Easily distracted was a recurring theme in his school reports. He's a lot like a puppy, jumping from one thing to the next without stopping, taking your breath away with his exuberance, but on the plus side, he is house trained, so no little accidents to clean up, unless he drinks too much lager and thinks your wardrobe is the loo – OMG, your pink suede shoes are in there!

As a child, Ben's dream was to be a professional football player (of course!) but again was distracted by anything or anyone walking by, so his eye was never on the ball, which is apparently quite important for a footballer. Then came karate (he couldn't give it a fair go due to the fear of hurting someone), learning the guitar to join a band, then he got bored after three weeks and gave it up to take up go-kart racing. Although he is the other side of thirty, he's still deciding what he wants to be when he grows up (if he grows up, which doesn't seem likely given his current laid-back attitude to responsibility). He is a skilled bricklayer and can turn his hand to pretty much anything from plumbing to installing a new kitchen. The problem, again, is he's easily distracted, so will rush of to fix Mrs Cartwright's leaking toilet while yours is half installed but not usable yet. Then he'll get a call about something else, and three weeks later, you're still waiting for him to return. Hopefully you have the option of a downstairs loo. And being self-employed, his lack of organisational skills with his paperwork has his accountant pulling her hair out. He turns up with a carrier bag full of receipts thrown in any old how. A filing system is anathema for him.

One thing I do need to mention: he's divorced (amicably) and has two children (adorable) and is probably the most devoted dad I know. He has the kids every weekend and often after school. He has never, to my knowledge, been late to pick them up or, worse still, got sidetracked elsewhere. His kids are his world, and I have the utmost respect for him as a parent. His life revolves around his family, Nana included, and I believe the family get-togethers are spectacular.

He's adorable but would he make a good husband? Well… if you're prepared to be the breadwinner, cleaner, organiser and only adult in the relationship, then yes. However, I wouldn't put money on him being on time for your wedding; he'll probably have had a call from his Auntie Audrey about a dripping tap and popped round to fix that on the way.

Charles

He's smart, unobtrusive and immaculately turned out. He gives the impression he's much older due to his commanding presence when he enters the room. Tall, but not too tall, slim and attractive in a serious looking way. Not an employee, obviously, Charles owns the place, you can tell. The suits suit him (sorry) and look like they're made for him, which they probably are. This is not a man who'll turn up in jogging bottoms or trainers.

Charles is the pair of Christian Louboutins you have always dreamt of. They may look amazing and be the most stylish things in the room, but they can really pinch your toes and you may find them very uncomfortable indeed; best to try before you buy.

His greying hair – well, silvering – gives him a distinguished appearance; the man has class oozing from every pore. He won't buy you half a lager in the Black Horse, he won't even ask what you'd like to drink; perfectly chilled Bollinger will arrive at your restaurant table in seconds, without any communication between Charles and the waiter.

Trouble is, he'll also tell you what you'd like to eat. Control freak may be a little strong, but this man is in charge, like it or lump it. Come to think of it, he didn't ask you out in the beginning, he just informed you he'd pick you up on Friday at eight. He has such charm and charisma you probably didn't even notice.

Your birthday will be amazing, no cosy night in with a takeaway and a bottle of Prosecco. He's booked dinner at the Ivy, tickets for the theatre, and a top London hotel. He's bought you flowers and they're not from Tesco, clearly. Sadly, he's also advised you what to wear, even suggested your favourite little black dress is perhaps a little too short, too tight or not really suitable! How rude, but it's all said in complete innocence, he genuinely has no clue what you're getting upset about, bless him.

Mother calls him 'Charlie darling', Pa calls him 'old chap'. Are you getting the picture? The parents live in the country, five dogs and any number of Range Rovers on the drive.

I do hope you had a good education, know which cutlery to use for the fish course, and your dad isn't a bus driver or you're out of the frame here.

Charles is, in fact, a very nice chap, if we can overlook the peculiarities, like telling you to run along and powder your nose when he takes an important phone call. He would be horrified if he upset or offended you, even more horrified if you made a fuss or got emotional. "Stiff upper lip, old girl, come on now, don't be a sillykins." It's the pat on the bum that's so bloody condescending, isn't it? He still believes it's okay to treat women as a lesser species, who can't really be expected to manage anything without his supervision. Can you imagine his face if the surgeon performing his vasectomy turns out to be a woman? Still, if you are a little bit ditzy and not overly bright, you may love being cosseted and protected from the real world. It's a bit like having a day out with your dad when you were six years old. He'll probably buy you an ice cream on the way home, if you're a good girl.

He's also very good at surprises; a weekend in Paris, eating at the best restaurants and a romantic dinner cruise down the Seine. Browsing in Montmartre, watching the artists touting for business. Don't get distracted and wander off, Charles has all the money, travel documents and your passport; you might lose it, probably best if Charles takes complete charge, in his opinion! You'll have some great adventures with him, he's warm, funny and spontaneous, always up for an impromptu get-together with friends – his friends, obviously.

He has leanings towards OCD, so if you're a bit messy, there may be tears before bedtime. Do not throw your coat over the back of the sofa, leave the top off the toothpaste, or not load the dishwasher in the most space-saving way. Charles always cleans the toilet after use and puts the seat down!

If you make it past first base, and the parents think you're an absolute sweetie, you'll get a fabulous diamond ring for the proposal that was his great-grandmother's. You'll hate it as it's so old-fashioned, but hey, Charles loves it, so that's okay then.

On the plus side, he won't mind your friends and is

happy for you to go out with them regularly. He probably won't even notice you're not there, he's far too busy reading *The Financial Times*. However, there may be conditions attached to attending social functions. He won't want your friend Stella to come to his birthday party, she has a nose piercing, wears those ghastly nail polish colours and laughs loudly at her own jokes; she's too full on, in his opinion! And never ever mention your uncle Norman, or his criminal record. I know what happened wasn't technically his fault, but Charles won't see it that way!

So, he's asked you, you've said yes (have you completely lost your mind?) and a date has been set. He will gently persuade you the wedding should take place at his favourite venue, probably a castle in Scotland, you should not cut your hair beforehand, it's best styled by his mother's hairdresser, and he MUST see a picture of the dress; after all, he knows what suits you. Is this a good time to ask yourself why he is not married? Good luck.

Charlie and the diamond factory

I'd known Charles from way back, when he was married to his second wife Miranda, an artist. It was glaringly obvious they weren't happy, and no one was surprised when she took off to live in Córdoba. Miranda had always been something of a free spirit, almost bohemian in her outlook. She would frequently fail to attend functions with Charles after becoming engrossed in her painting, much to his annoyance. She was a beautiful woman, with free-flowing auburn hair, delicate features and striking green eyes. I admired her; she had a passion for her work that took her over, but sadly left little room for anything else, including Charles, who is not a man who takes kindly to feeling second best to anything or anyone.

I felt a little sorry for Charles, if I'm honest. Although his public persona is that of a strong man, I sensed something vulnerable in him. After a few drinks one evening at an event we were both attending, he admitted he felt a bit of a failure. He had several thriving businesses, but two failed marriages, no children, and was questioning his purpose on the planet. "What's the point of all this, Hannah? What is the point of working my bloody backside off? I have no one with whom to share the fruits, as it were. And no one to hand over to." I reassured him to the best of my ability that things would get better, he'd meet someone new, and they would love him. I listed his good characteristics, and with a level of sincerity I didn't know I possessed, told him that any woman would be proud to be his partner. To be fair, he is strikingly handsome, with beautiful, if sad, blue eyes and elegant hands.

A few weeks later, I had been press-ganged into watching my friend's son play football when Charles appeared out of nowhere at my side, holding out a paper cup full of steaming, frothy hot chocolate. As the weather was appalling, with driving rain and a very chilly wind, it was gratefully received. "I wanted to thank you again for your kind words last time we met. I'm afraid I was being somewhat melancholy, and you were, and are, a breath of fresh air, so thank you. And if I may be so bold, I'd be delighted if you would do me the honour of accepting an invitation to dinner? I have the perfect venue in mind, you'll love it."

Who even talks like that? I had to give my face a quick talking to, so as not to giggle. And my brain was telling my mouth to respond with 'My dear chap, what an absolutely darling idea! I'd be delighted to accompany you to dinner'. What I think I actually said was, "There's a new tapas restaurant just opened opposite Berties on the high street. I'd love to try that, if you fancy it?" Which, by amazing coincidence, was the venue he already had in mind.

After confirming my likes (just about everything) and my dislikes (olives), Charles proceeded to order an amazing selection of tapas, in fluent Spanish, of course, which from some people may seem pretentious, but I'm a sucker for a foreign language. Embarrassingly for Charles, the waiter's Spanish was virtually non-existent, which I found hilarious but managed to keep a lid on so as not to offend him.

The whole evening – and the champagne – flowed seamlessly. This was a man who seemed to be good at everything, attentive without being pushy, chatty, interested and interesting. We talked about a wide range of topics, from work to families and everything in between. He had a great sense of humour, too. In saying that, maybe it was his impeccable manners that meant he laughed at my one-liners. At the end of the evening, without a hint of sarcasm, he told me he found me refreshingly different (from whom, I wondered, the rest of humanity?), delightful company and asked if I'd care to repeat the experience. Hell, yeah! And no, that wasn't what I actually said. I politely said I would love to and gave him my number. The taxi I hadn't noticed him order appeared from nowhere and he handed the driver the fare and an eye-watering tip, instructing the driver to make sure I not only got home safely, but to wait until I was in the house before leaving.

The following morning, an enormous bouquet of flowers was delivered to my house (I work from home a lot of the time). Completely white flowers, which I had revealed during our conversation the previous evening as my favourite. The card read: 'Thank you for a delightful evening, hope to see you soon C xx'

The dates that followed were always fun, in a subdued, sophisticated way. No karaoke nights at the pub with the girls, which I missed, but I met some of his friends, who were all charming and welcoming. There were dinners, black-tie events, theatre trips, weekends away in posh country hotels and a long weekend in Rome. My credit card took a beating, and my wardrobe was so full it resembled my stomach after a five-course meal, but I was having the time of my life.

Then he called to invite me to a race meeting. Not just any old meeting, but Ladies' Day at Royal Ascot. Panic set in. I had maxed out on the credit card, so what to do? I called Lou, my old school friend who owns a quirky little boutique in Elmhurst. I love that woman! She shut up shop early on the following Monday, and we spent a couple of hours drinking wine while I tried on almost everything in the shop. Lou has an incredible talent of knowing what will suit anyone; she produced things I wouldn't have ever considered that looked amazing. We agreed on the most stunning red dress that made me look ten pounds lighter and three inches taller, with dainty matching strappy sandals. When I asked the price, my heart sank all the way to my boots. It was not an option. Lou was determined I was to wear it, and insisted I take it and pay her a monthly repayment. She's such a lovely friend.

I probably owe her more than the price of the dress and shoes. When Charles came to pick me up, his eyes widened and he said, "When we get married, you must wear red, you look absolutely stunning." I laughed, of course; I had no idea he was serious. Royal Ascot was incredible, a different world. Charles placed bets on my behalf, as I had no idea what to do, and on the way home passed me an envelope with five hundred pounds in. "Your winnings, my dear. Beginner's luck, they say." I argued that I had won nothing, as he had placed bets for me with his money and it became a little heated. Even though it would have been a chance to repay Lou over half the debt, I could not and would not accept it. Charles laughed at me, and said I was overly principled, but let it go.

The following Sunday, we had lunch with his parents, who were both lovely and welcoming. We ate at the Regency Hotel, which was another awakening for me. Lunch for the four of us cost more than my Ascot outfit.

Charles called both his parents by their Christian names, which I found a bit odd, but I was invited to do the same. His mother, Diana, had a low-key chat with me when the men were talking business over coffee.

"I'm delighted to make your acquaintance, my dear, and it's wonderful to see Charlie so happy. After Miranda left, I was worried about him, but you are just what he needs. She was beautiful, and a lovely woman, but Charlie needs someone who will put him first and I think you'll be very good for him. I do hope, in the fullness of time, you and I will become good friends. Who knows, we may end up wedding dress shopping together, eh?" and she winked. It's rare that I'm speechless, but I was then.

As it happens, she was right. I think I was flattered to be asked when he proposed, and although I believe he loved me, he was heavily influenced by Diana, who I had come to like very much. My engagement ring was a family heirloom, diamonds twisted into a huge knot. I found it heavy and cumbersome but didn't want to appear rude, so I said nothing. I did wonder if Miranda had also worn it. My wedding dress was not red, but a soft cream with a lot of lace and heavily beaded. Diana agreed to Lou coming with us to choose the dress, who is a little more forthright than me, and I knew she'd never let me wear anything that she didn't think looked fantastic. Again, it was not my choice, or Lou's, but Diana's, who had thought my first choice a little understated. There was no hen night; Charles didn't really approve of the concept, so I went back to the tapas bar with the girls the weekend before, and we had a sedate evening as fitting being engaged to Charles.

The day of the wedding passed in a blur; if I'm being honest, I was very happy but also a little apprehensive, and I couldn't put my finger on why. Diana and her husband Clive had given me a stunning diamond necklace and bracelet, which I wrongly assumed was just to wear for the wedding. I was informed it was, "Just a little welcome to the family gift." We'd decided on a small, informal wedding, about fifty guests in the gardens of the Regency Hotel. The weather was perfect. Although I only remember bits of the day, I clearly remember hugging my girlfriends goodbye and Lou saying, "Have an amazing time in Venice and take good care of yourself."

To which Charles responded immediately, "Worry not, dearest Louisa, I will take very good care of her, she won't need to worry her pretty little head about a thing." Sometimes he sounded like a Shakespearian character and could come across as a tad overbearing.

It was on our honeymoon that Charles suggested for the first time I should consider giving up work, as there was no need for us both to be stressed and busy all the time. I thought he was joking, but he never joked about work. I brushed it off and forgot all about it.

The months after the wedding flew by. I moved into Charles' house, and we talked about whether to rent out my house or sell it. Charles was of the opinion I should sell up and put the money in a little account to help fund my apparent shoe obsession. I thought it better to rent it out to top up my salary (I was beginning to feel uncomfortable with the inequality in our finances, and Charles refusing money towards the household bills, etc.).

Money was the cause of our first serious argument. On the one hand, he was refusing to let me pay for anything at all, which did not sit comfortably with me. On the other hand, eyebrows were raised when I bought a handbag, a pair of shoes or even a plant for the hallway – from my own account, I might add.

"When you give up work, I'm happy to give you a small allowance for these sorts of things, but I do feel you should have asked me if we needed this green spiky thing taking up half the hallway. And as for those ghastly cushions for the lounge, they're cheap and tacky and I'm afraid you'll need to return those."

I was hurt, especially as I had collected the cushions from my house and not bought them. And unfortunately, when hurt, I manage to translate that into anger, which is not a good look. Charles looked horrified when I tore him off a strip and asked if I would mind lowering my voice (the neighbours!) and refraining from the rather colourful language. My response was even uglier. " F--- the bloody neighbours, Charles, and F--- you too, you're a patronising prick!" and I burst into tears.

To his credit, he put an arm around me and guided me to the sofa. "I think we should gather ourselves, have a nice cup of coffee, and see if we can't talk this through in a calm manner." So far, so good. "Off you pop and get us some coffee, darling, I have a couple of calls to make, and we'll sort things out, okay?"

See what I was up against? Every time there was any kind of disagreement, I felt like I was a four-year-old that had thrown a tantrum. After yet another stupid row after me buying the wrong toilet roll – a cheaper version of the one Charles preferred – I sat at the bottom of the stairs with my head in my hands. When he asked why I was sitting there, I replied, "You treat me like a child, so I've put myself on the naughty step."

We struggled on for eighteen months until, one day, after a very stressful day at work, I called in to see Lou on the way home. We had a couple of drinks, and I stayed around an hour. Lou repeatedly asked me what was up – sixth sense, I think, as I had said nothing about Charles at all. I brushed it off as work issues, gave her a hug and left, after arranging to meet up the following week. I had sent Charles a text message, saying I'd be late home, and where I was, so was blown away by the reaction when I got home.

"Firstly, it is very disrespectful to just decide not to come straight home when I'm expecting you, and yes, I know you sent a text message, but I may have made arrangements for us this evening. Secondly, I feel you let your job and your friends take priority over me, which is just not on. And thirdly, I'm not a particular fan of your friend Louisa. I feel she is a bad influence on you, and I won't have you dragged down to her level, with her drinking and so on. The less you see of her, the better."

"Are you f---ing serious? Who the f--- do you think you are?" I was furious.

"I rest my case. An hour with the lovely Louisa and here

we go again, raising your voice and using foul language. You, young lady – and I use the term loosely – need to remember which side your bread is buttered."

I mumbled something about not liking bread anyway, picked up my handbag and left the house. The sad realisation dawned that I had married an opinionated control freak. While that description has been applied to me occasionally – probably accurately – at that moment, I decided that the only opinionated control freak I wanted to spend my life with was me.

Danny

Oh dear! I hope you're a confident person who doesn't worry what your man is doing while he's not with you, poor Danny just can't help himself. That's just the point, he does help himself, to other people's girlfriends mainly. He's so good looking and magnetic, these women just fall at his feet. Danny is the sparkly strappy silver sandals you bought for the Christmas party but never wore again as they are so uncomfortable. The heel snapped off anyway, so they should go in the bin. Beautiful shoes to look at but not wearable, if you get my drift.

He was born into a house full of women, youngest child and only son to Barbie, a petite, stunning woman whose husband left when Danny was six months old. His three older sisters, his mother and Danny lived with Barbie's mother to make ends meet and he was adored, fussed over, told he was cute and spoilt rotten all his life. To be fair, he is cute. How can you stay angry with this Adonis, blond hair hanging provocatively over one eye, smiling at you with those puppy-dog eyes.

How could you not fall in love with Danny? Everyone does, some of them still nursing a broken heart years later.

Don't think he's shallow, he really does believe you're the love of his life, until Jessica Jones struts by in her micro mini skirt with legs up to her armpits!

A short attention span, his teachers said. As soon as he gets what he wants, he doesn't want it anymore, and if he can't get what he wants, oh well, he'll find something easier to get. If you have it, Danny wants it and will do whatever it takes to get it. I blame Barbie, really. From day one it was the same: "Oh, give Danny a biscuit, love. Oh, it's the last one? Give it to Danny, love, he's only little, he doesn't understand."

So, Danny gets to choose which bedroom he sleeps in, what Barbie cooks for dinner, what the family watch on the TV, and which girl he's going to target next.

Okay, what are his good points? Ummm…

He's cute, very cute. He's attractive, very attractive. He's always smiling (so would I be if I got everything I wanted) and he's cute, did I mention that already? His lopsided grin could melt the snow from 100 metres away, and he's irresistible, women just want to look after him. There's so much of the child in him, it's inevitable, I suppose.

It's not just his looks that appeal, he's magnetic in every way. Even as a kid, when the local beat bobby caught him with a pocketful of eight packets of Smarties that he'd stolen from the newsagents, he just told Danny he really should pay for them next time. Not even a threat of telling his mum or making him take them back to the shop. Luckily, he didn't make a career out of shoplifting after that.

Talking of careers, he doesn't have one, or even a job

just at the moment. It's not easy to hold down a job when you're late most days, ignore your customers in favour of chatting up Carrie Parker, and forget to bank the takings. But Barbie and the girls don't seem to mind. "That's our Danny, love him," is their response to any criticism of him.

You'll never be short of friends with him, but they'll also be your competition. Bees round a honey pot, they call it. That endearing smile and his youthful exuberance makes you want to be a part of it, albeit a short-lived, small part.

He's not a snappy dresser, never been one to follow the pack or care too much what others think. Casual but clean, and beautifully ironed, by Barbie or one of his sisters, obviously. Jeans are his wardrobe staple, usually with a white T-shirt that's past its best, and those soft brown boots… did I mention this man is cute?

So, is he potential marriage material? Not in a million billion years, in my opinion, but if your heart is made of stone, and you're okay with someone hogging the mirror all the time, he's worth dating for as long as you can hold his attention.

Good luck!

The Danny disaster

It was not something I had anticipated, nor was it an experience I wished to repeat. From the beginning, dating Danny was an exercise in navigating an unpredictable storm. His charm, which initially seemed endearing, quickly revealed itself to be a façade for his erratic behaviour and poor relationship skills.

I'm not sure exactly how we got together but I know alcohol was involved. After a very lively evening in the Rose and Crown, celebrating Teresa's birthday, I found myself perched on the edge of a table in the smoking area outside the pub – not that I smoke, of course, so stop judging me – with Danny tying up my bootlaces after I'd taken a little tumble going to the toilets. Gazing drunkenly into his eyes, the spell was cast, and I was under it. The man I had fallen for, in less than a nanosecond, turned out to be someone totally unstable, unreliable and unsuitable. It is true what they say about not making a decision while under the influence. I would also advise against dating someone that you know has a bit of a bad reputation for his romantic liaisons, but you know me, ever the optimist, thinking he'll be different with me. It has been said that I have a tendency to see the glass more than half full; in fact, I think I see it overflowing on occasion. At this point in my life, although I'd taken a few knocks, I certainly had never suffered from a broken heart; moreover, I was probably a little overconfident that it could never happen to me. Having spent many an evening consoling friends sobbing into their Prosecco over some man or other, I smugly thought they were a bit silly to get so ensnared in a serious relationship. Pride comes before a fall and all that.

Danny was often late for a date, sometimes up to an hour, occasionally failing to turn up at all. He once sent his friend instead with some lame excuse about working late so was unable to contact me. When he did show up, he was often distracted or constantly checking his phone. When I did manage to get his full attention, he was charming, great fun and very tactile, if you get my drift. And remember, I was completely under his spell and besotted with him, so was not thinking clearly. Things took a positive turn, or so I believed, when he got a job working away and was only home every third weekend or so. Of course, he needed to see his family and friends in his valuable free time, so he'd often show up on a Friday evening with a holdall full of laundry for me to sort and I may not see him again until Sunday morning, after I'd cooked him breakfast and washed and ironed his clothes. I know what you're thinking, 'wake up, girl, this man is stringing you along', and you're right, of course, I know that now.

Wake up I did, and it was a rude awakening for sure. One Sunday morning, Danny had turned up after having been to the gym, or so I believed. He went for a shower while I cooked him a full English and left his phone on the dining table. When it pinged with a text message, I innocently glanced at it, only to see the beginning of a message from Sammie-Jo: 'Hey sexy, you left your keys here xxx'

Yes, he had certainly been doing a workout, but with Sammie-Jo. I happen to know a Sammie-Jo, there aren't many people with that name, so I correctly assumed it was the one I knew, the barmaid in the Rose and Crown. Of course, when challenged, he desperately tried to talk his way out of it, but I'm not as stupid as I obviously had been and I'm ashamed to admit, I lost the plot somewhat. Breakfast ended up on the wall and the floor and I threw him and his bag of freshly laundered clothes out of the front door. Having been told I was delusional and a mad woman, I sadly agreed he had a point on both counts. Delusional to think we had a special relationship, and mad to have not seen what was right under my nose.

Ed

Ed is odd. Sorry if that sounds a little harsh, but I can't find a more suitable word. Not necessarily odd in a bad way, just odd. Maybe 'different' would be kinder, but odd it is. Personally, I have often wondered if he's a different species, an alien plant from the planet Gribble sent to study humanity. He is the weirdest lime-green lace-up shoes I wouldn't be seen dead in even if it was snowing. Anyway, I digress.

So, what do we know about Ed? Well, that's my point, we don't. Does he have family? Who knows? He lives in a nice neighbourhood, in a ground-floor flat next door to the vet's in Moore Street. Alone. No pets, not many visitors, nothing to make him stand out or be noticed. Is he shy, perhaps? Nope, always smiles and says hello if he sees you in the supermarket.

Where did he come from? Not round here, no one his age remembers him from school. He was just there, snuck in quietly without anyone noticing.

He's possibly in his thirties, I think. I've begged Claire, the receptionist at the doctor's surgery, to check his age but she's far too professional to breach patient confidentiality. Says it's more than her job's worth, and she is a jobsworth, if you ask me!

He's average height and build, not a looker in the conventional sense, but he has a certain something I can't really put my finger on. He likes animals, though. He once stopped in the park to stroke Carole Fisher's dog and it didn't bite him, so animals must like him too, which makes him okay in my book. (Carole Fisher's bloody dog has bitten, or at least tried to bite, almost everyone else I can think of. Except the postman, strangely, and now Ed.)

He's a conventional but casual dresser – jeans, T-shirt, hoodie and normal shoes – and seems comfortable in his own skin, if you know what I mean. But there's just that something I'm struggling to put a label on. The oddness. Just too much nothingness, no family anyone has ever seen, no obvious friends and no social life. He goes to the pub, but alone. He chats briefly to the bar staff, acknowledges the familiar faces, has a couple of beers and goes home. Doesn't seem interested in the football on the pub TV, doesn't seem interested in any of the local eye candy, either male or female. Don't you think he's odd?

So, I'm looking for something to say about Ed, and to be frank, it's not easy. I mean, what does he do to earn a living? We have no idea. He doesn't seem to work regular hours, comes and goes all hours of the day and night but clearly earns enough to drive that fabulous black Mercedes convertible and he shops in Waitrose. Okay, he's not short of money but his flat is minimally furnished according to Rosa Mundy, and she's the only one I know who's been in there. She says it looks like he just moved in and hasn't had a chance to unpack any personal items yet. I'm surprised he let her in, knocking on his door to ask if he's ever broken into someone's house, with some cock and bull story about having locked herself out and being too short to climb over the fence to get in the back way. He gallantly lent her a stepladder to get over the fence with a wry smile – he could see from his flat that her front door was open. That woman gives the rest of us a bad name, honestly, she's so transparent.

I know he likes liquorice toffee, and Weetabix, and he uses eco-friendly washing detergent. He also uses Waitrose extra soft toilet tissue in white and is not a vegetarian. Okay, so I sort of stalked him a little on Saturday; it's not my fault we happened to be in Waitrose at the same time. Yes, I did shop on Friday in Tesco, but you never remember everything on the list, do you? And I needed some apricots soaked in Madeira urgently.

Sometimes I've seen him walking in the park, with a faraway look on his face, almost sad, wistful. Maybe he's thinking about the planet Gribble and missing his family. Or maybe he has a girlfriend there. He sits on a bench for a while, just gazing vacantly into the lake as if it contains the answers to the meaning of life.

So, if this mysterious man appeals to you, I wish you all the luck in the world with your quest to catch his eye. And please, if you do get lucky, let us in on Ed and his secret life. Thank you.

P.S. OMG! I feel terrible. How did I turn into someone so awful? The things I've said about that poor man! I'm so judgemental. I've just seen Carole in the queue at the post office (you know Carole with the extremely grumpy dog, which, for your interest, is called Norman! Ridiculous name for a dog!). Anyway, she was in the park earlier, Norman decided to run off with some kid's ball, Carole chased him and slipped on the path, breaking her wrist in the process. So, the reason I'm telling you this, she had to go to A & E for an X-ray, etc., and who is the lovely doctor who treats her? Yep, only Ed the mysterious.

Never had Carole down as a gossip, but she's clearly been taking lessons from Rosa Mundy. She asked the nurse who fitted her with a beautiful pink plaster cast (pink! Really?) about the doctor. Apparently, Ed the mysterious transferred to our hospital three years ago after a terrible tragedy. His wife and child were hit by a drunk driver on the way home from school and Ed was on duty in A & E where they lived in Hartlepool. The team were unable to save either of them. Ed couldn't face working there after that. Note to self, never judge a book by its cover. I'm truly sorry, Ed. And I think the nurse who repeated the story should be disciplined; has that poor man not been through enough without people gossiping about his private life?

Note to self: stop being nosey about people, don't indulge in gossip, and never make assumptions. I'm truly sorry, Ed.

Fraser

raser is navy blue. Not literally, obviously, but it's how I view him. Not severe enough to be black, or lively enough to be red or green, but serviceable in a 'your mother will love him' kind of way. Navy blue, mid-price court shoes is Fraser.

He'll fit into any situation or occasion with ease, laid back without seeming indifferent or uninterested. Confident but not arrogant, I rather like him.

He grew up in a modest four-bed semi on the outskirts of town and went to the old grammar school along with his younger brother Kevin. His father was in business, something financial I believe, and his mother worked as a receptionist for a privately run children's and family therapy centre. Nice people, the whole family. God, I hate the word nice, but it does fit them.

My first encounter with Fraser was in Starbucks, when he collected his coffee (soya milk latte, I seem to recall) and stepped back onto my left foot with gusto. I shrieked and he spun round and subsequently poured most of the latte all over my other foot. Not intentionally, of course, but in a fluster. His apology went on for some time; he even offered to replace my shoes, which were the most awful off-white, scuffed and battered pumps that I usually only wore in the garden. I'm not sure who was the most embarrassed, him about nearly breaking my toes and scalding me, or me that I'd been caught in those ghastly shoes. We ended up laughing about the whole episode.

My friend Millie dated him for a while after university, but it ended when he went travelling for a year. She still speaks very highly of him; in fact, I secretly think she married his brother Kevin to be close to Fraser, but we'll keep that to ourselves.

He's good looking, in a young George Clooney kind of way, with amazing teeth. I do so like a man with nice teeth, which is maybe because he's a dentist. Can a dentist do his own teeth, I wonder? He has a partner, as in at his dental practice, not as in girlfriend, and they're based at the end of Moore St, near the vet's where Ed lives. I use the dental surgery in town, so have never had the pleasure of having Fraser fiddling about with me, so to speak, but I may consider moving!

Anyway, back to the navy blue. He has plenty of personality; great fun without being over the top. Good sense of humour, a little over 6'1", and all his own hair and teeth! He always looks smartly put together, crisp white shirt, dark jeans and a blazer. Slim build, a great smile and dimples. Dark hair with a sprinkling of silver around the temples. Why haven't I tried to ensnare him, I ask myself. Well, he's very nice, and nice men aren't really my thing, it seems. My experience with men is like my experience of apples: I pick a gorgeous shiny one, crisp, juicy and full of flavour, but when I bite into it, it's slightly bruised and has the remains of a maggot inside.

He has a wide range of interests and hobbies. He once played rugby at county level but, after a nasty tackle when he broke his ankle, had to retire from competitive sport at that level. He still has a slight limp. He does play squash, and tennis in the summer. Great legs, by the way.

Personally, I think he's a good catch for someone. He's smart, funny, fit and, apart from his shellfish allergy, great company over dinner. Ask Millie about the shellfish allergy, she never forgave herself for accidentally poisoning him that summer. Oh, and he can cook, too. When I say he can cook, I mean he makes Gordon Ramsay look like an amateur. Apparently, his beef wellington is out of this world. And his chocolate mousse is so soft and silky you could sleep in it, but that would be messy. To be fair, a lot of this information is second hand, from Millie, and I think even though she's happily married to his brother, she secretly still has a bit of a thing for him.

Yep, he's definitely worth trying for size.

Giovanni
(pronounced Gee-o-vahhh-nee)

May I present Giovanni, who would like to introduce himself to you. "Hello, pretty lay-dee, my name is Giovanni and I come from Napoli in Eetalee. I am very 'andsome and charming, no? I think you are already a leetle in love with me, I can see eet in your oh so bee-you-tiful eyes."

Run, girls, run for the hills. This one is so in love with himself no one can get a look in. (I have heard a rumour that his real name is George and he's originally from Wolverhampton, but let's not spoil his big moment.) Giovanni is the plasticky red high heels with diamante bits stuck on the front, the ones that even the charity shop can't sell.

George – sorry, I mean Giovanni – lives in town with Mamma, who is a big figure in his life, in every way. Mamma is only 5'2" tall but I think rotund probably describes her best. She walks as though one leg is shorter than the other, with a waddle almost. She cooks for him, does all his washing, cleans his room and interrogates any female under the age of fifty that comes anywhere near her precious bambino. Giovanni is her pride and joy, and it shows. When she tells you about him, she has a smile that is as wide as the Thames and would light up the room, apart from her three remaining black teeth.

There is a rumour that his papa, Giovanni Senior, was involved in some rather shady business dealings and was shot dead by some even dodgier people. Personally, I think our Giovanni put that one out to impress the girls.

To be honest, he is attractive in an almost feminine way. Long, curly, dark locks, always shining, and huge velvety brown eyes that a girl could drown in. He's not tall by any means, but certainly a good few inches taller than Mamma. And charm? By the bucketload if you fall for that sort of nonsense. And he wears a little too much gold for my taste, a heavy-duty chain around his neck, a bracelet so heavy I think it's part of his gym regime to lift his arm, and a compulsory earring.

But it is for you to decide if he's your ideal man, so I'll try and be objective.

He's certainly attentive on a date, asking lots of questions about you. "Can you cook? Proper pasta? How's your risotto? Are you good at keeping the house nice?"

He'll also want to know if you have any brothers, are they sporty? He's halfway to dumping you already, just checking your brothers won't chase him out of town and beat the crap out of him.

You probably wouldn't want to set up home with him, unless you can afford a house with at least two bathrooms and an annexe for Mamma. I can't see him leaving her any time soon. She'll spend the rest of her life reminding him how handsome he is and overseeing any potential relationships to make certain he's treated like a king. He does spend a great deal of time in front of the mirror, often telling himself how gorgeous he is. It puts me in mind of the Carly Simon song 'You're So Vain', he probably thinks this book is about him.

He's also quite lazy; used to having Mamma as his personal maid, he'll expect the same from you. It's funny, I've often heard some of my married with 2.4 children friends saying that a husband is just a large child, and they don't want any more! This is the man that will send you up for a relaxing bath after a very long day, then call you because the baby is crying five minutes after you got in the tub.

Your friends will love him, he's all over them like chicken pox, telling them how bee-you-tiful they are too. Just remember not to let him give them a lift home, it could be awkward for all parties. Anyway, that's not likely to happen, he will have probably consumed several glasses of Pinot Grigio with the terrible pasta you spent all afternoon making and can't drive.

There must be someone who will love him, despite my observations, but if I'm honest, I can't imagine who. She would have a lot to contend with: Mamma being a permanent fixture, Giovanni's eye for the ladies, and probably having to wait on him hand and foot. Throw a couple of kids into the mix, and from my perspective anyway, a life of drudgery. I mean, he has some admirable qualities: he clearly adores Mamma, even carries her groceries home so she doesn't have to struggle on the bus. But whether you'd ever get him to yourself is another matter. I think you'd be a third wheel under constant scrutiny, which does not sound like fun to me.

So, what does Giovanni have going for him, really? Oh, I forgot, he is very 'andsome and charming and you're already a leetle in love with him, aren't you?

Howard

Poor Howard, he's a sweetie but he has had a rough time. Not so much in recent years but his childhood was pretty tough to say the least. I visualise Howard as my Birkenstocks. I bought them long before they were fashionable, I thought they were ugly but sensible and, somehow, they've become one of my most comfortable items of footwear, and a bit trendy into the bargain.

Having red hair and freckles made Howard an obvious target for bullies at school. He was also a little heavier than most boys his age, and what was his mother thinking calling him Howard and hand-knitting his school jumpers? These days she'd have social services on her doorstep for such crimes. It was never going to end well.

Since the age of six, the school nasties would casually stroll over, ask his name, and when he told them would laugh uproariously and shout, "How 'ard? This 'ard, mate!" and punch or kick him as hard as they could. He spent many nights crying himself to sleep, dreading every day that followed. It took its toll, exhaustion causing him to often fall asleep at school, giving the bullies a chance to tip his chair back so he'd fall on the floor. He comforted himself with extra helpings of his mother's delicious homemade sponge and custard, except for treacle sponge, which reminded him of his hair due to the colour. Consequently, Howard became seriously overweight, not only a health worry but making any PE lessons another nightmare to be endured. An only child, too, there was no supportive big brother to fight his corner. A lonely and very unhappy time for a kid. Then the long prayed-for miracle happened. At thirteen, Howard started to grow taller, a lot taller. As a result, he slimmed down, or at least his weight was distributed more evenly. By fifteen, he was the tallest in his year, and average to slightly above-average build. He started playing basketball with a family who'd moved in next door and discovered he was pretty good at it. PE was still not his favourite subject, but not the embarrassing torture it used to be. The bullies backed off; not completely, but his new stature made them a little fearful. If he hit back, they may get hurt.

The kids next door were still his only real friends; all younger than Howard, he saw himself as an older brother to them, always available to play with them, listen to their woes and was often their babysitter. They lived with their father who worked long hours to provide the best he could for them since their mother had run off with a neighbour's husband years ago. Howard's view was to see himself as very fortunate to have such a great mother and felt deeply for these three children. I told you he's a sweetie.

In the early hours of one November morning, just after Howard's fifteenth birthday, he awoke to a terrible smell of burning and a peculiar orange glow in his bedroom.

Half asleep, he had thought he was having a dream that his dreaded hair was on fire but quickly realised it was coming from outside the house, next door, in fact. Shouting to his mother to call the fire service, he ran out of the back door, vaulted the fence and looked up at the window at the back of next door's house. Three faces, barely distinguishable, were pressed up against the glass, tears streaming. "Open the window, I'm coming to get you!" he shouted. By the time he'd climbed up and into the room, he could barely breathe himself. The smoke was pouring in under the door and he knew there was only one way out. Thankfully, the emergency services were now on the scene and Howard lowered each child to safety before collapsing on the floor of the room. After a dramatic rescue, he was taken to hospital with smoke inhalation and burns to his feet.

His only concern was for the children who thankfully recovered well, as did their father who had been asleep downstairs, which probably saved his life.

'Howard the Hero' screamed the headline in the local paper.

"How hard was it to climb up there?" people asked. For the first time, Howard smiled at the play on his name.

What happened to Howard since then? He left school and joined the fire service, obviously. He's a hero every day.

There have been girlfriends, all shorter than him as he's now 6'3" tall. He's a quiet guy, unassuming and kind. He loves children and animals and gives regular fire safety talks at his old school.

Not long after joining the fire service, his mother was diagnosed with cancer and Howard put his new career on hold to care for her. He was there for every appointment, scan and chemotherapy session. In the last months, with help from a cancer charity, Howard did not leave her side, putting his own life on hold to make hers as comfortable as possible.

Sadly, his mother died, but Howard was with her at the end, holding her hand and being the wonderful man he'd become. Her funeral was obviously sad, and Howard was overwhelmed with the love and support from friends, neighbours and his colleagues. A celebration of the life of the woman who had single-handedly raised this amazing man.

He now shares a flat with two colleagues from work and, in his spare time, raises money for cancer charities running marathons!

He's a good man; you could do a lot worse.

Howard heads home

I loved Howard. Unfortunately, I loved holidays more. In many ways, Howard was my perfect boyfriend: kind, funny, considerate and always there with a hug when I was going through one of my regular meltdowns over whatever my latest drama was.

Howard and I met at an awards ceremony where Howard had been nominated for an outstanding act of courage award for the dramatic rescue of two small children and their dog from the canal. He was off duty at the time and had been out walking Poppy, his dog, when the two little ones had fallen from a canal boat. Their mother was hysterically screaming, as neither she nor the children could swim. Heaven knows how the dog ended up in there, but Howard turned into Superman and got them all to safety, with the help of some passers-by. He was so humble on receipt of the award, saying anyone would have done the same, and was mortified when the local paper ran the headline 'Howard the hero strikes again', retelling the house fire story from years before too; he's not big on being in the limelight.

Being with Howard was easy. He quickly became like my favourite Birkenstocks, warm, comfortable and just what I needed after a long day in high heels. Before the year was out, we had moved in together. He cooked, he cleaned, he tolerated my whining about work on an almost daily basis with good grace, in fact, there didn't seem to be any negatives at all. Until, that is, the subject of our first holiday together came up. I had been scrolling through the internet for days: Corfu, Cyprus and so on. When I presented Howard with the three locations I had narrowed it down to, he shook his head. "I was thinking Wales, there is so much beautiful scenery, or maybe the Peak District? Or how about Cornwall?" And so, our first real argument began, and yes, I did turn into a princess pretty quickly.

"I don't work all the hours God sends to take my summer holiday in some bloody forest in the middle of nowhere where it will pour with rain every bloody day. I need bars, restaurants, people, and days just laying on a beach soaking up the sun!" Howard simply raised an eyebrow at my outburst. The argument (my side) and the level-headed discussion (his side) continued for days. We finally agreed to both compromise, the first week in Ayia Napa doing my kind of holiday, then Cornwall for the second week, although I drew the line at staying in a tent. I mean, where would I plug in my GHDs?

I'm not proud of myself here, but I guess you need to know what happened. The first week was amazing, the weather was fantastic, the beaches were beautiful with crystal clear water, and the nights were one long crazy party. Howard spent some of the afternoons on the beach with me, but most mornings, he took himself off, while I was sleeping off a tiny hangover. Apparently, there's a fascinating monastery and museum, and lots of beautiful churches. Shame I missed those. In the evenings, we had dinner together, but when I suggested heading on to some of the bars, he acquiesced for an hour or two, before pleading a headache due to the loud music. We had made friends with a few other Brits, so I partied with them into the wee small hours and left Howard to his early nights. On the flight home, we had another argument, with me accusing Howard of being a middle-aged bore, and him telling me it was like holidaying with an unruly teenager. We got home, showered, slept for an hour, and, leaving our sun-kissed packed suitcases in the hallway, picked up our pre-packed Cornwall bags and set off, with Poppy, for our next adventure.

It did rain, and for two of the days we endured gale-force winds. In a caravan, that's quite testing. Howard took Poppy for long bracing walks in the rain, while I sulked in the caravan, pretending to read my book. I was horrified when I realised Howard was expecting us to cook most nights in the caravan too. There was a restaurant of sorts, and a couple of pubs in the nearest village, but Howard thought cooking together would be fun. Well, it's not fun to do on holiday exactly what you do at home. I told you I was a princess.

The next few weeks after we returned home, we carried on as before, without really talking about the holiday. But I felt something had changed and I couldn't think how to recapture what we'd had, until I had a brainwave. I checked his work rota for the first long weekend he was free and booked us a romantic trip to Paris. A five-star hotel almost on the banks of the Seine, tickets for the Louvre, a dinner cruise on the river, I pulled out all the stops and almost maxed out my credit card. Obviously, Howard was delighted, apart from the fact I had forgotten to check availability of his cousin to have Poppy, which, as it turned out, was a problem that weekend. Howard point-blank refused to put the dog in kennels for any reason ever, so that caused a few cross words. Fortunately, Howard's friend Alan stepped in and saved the day on that one.

So, we set sail – actually, we flew into Paris – on the Friday afternoon, both excited for the trip. First problem, the hotel was 'a bit flash', apparently. There's no pleasing some people, I found myself muttering. Secondly, the food in the hotel restaurant was French. What was he expecting, pie and mash? Don't get me wrong, apparently, he was not complaining or being ungrateful, just not keen on French food.

As it turned out, he wasn't overly enamoured with Paris in general: full of tourists, too many people, very expensive, even the weather didn't meet expectations. As for very expensive, well for goodness' sake, a) it's flipping Paris, what did he expect? And b) I was paying for everything anyhow. We did all the touristy things, with Howard grumbling about the queues, and finally I snapped.

"If it's that bad, why don't you quit moaning about it and just bloody go home?" So, he did. Just turned on his heel and walked off. At first, I thought he'd just gone back to the hotel, so I treated myself to a coffee and the most expensive croissant I'd ever had and sat watching the artists in Montmartre. I'd hoped we'd get a romantic sketch of the two of us, so out of spite and princessy-ness, I paid fifty euros for a little charcoal drawing of myself looking melancholy. That would remind him that he'd made me miserable on our romantic trip to Paris, I thought to myself. After sitting for an hour reflecting on everything that had happened since we'd got to Paris, I realised I had probably been quite selfish again, expecting him to enjoy my type of holiday without giving any consideration to his feelings. Determined to put things right, I set off at a brisk pace for the hotel before realising I had no idea where I was and no idea how to get back to the hotel. After half an hour,

I not only had a nasty blister but also a realisation that I was right back where I started. I gave in and found a taxi. On arrival in the foyer, I realised that I didn't have a room key, but the receptionist was eagerly awaiting my arrival.

"Madame, the monsieur, he ask me to give you this," and handed me my room key and a sealed envelope with, it must be said, a somewhat smug expression. After resisting – with some difficulty – an urge to slap her stupid face, I took myself up to our room with a sense of overwhelming dread. Howard was not there, and I knew, without checking the bathroom or the wardrobe, that none of his belongings were there either. Inside the envelope was my passport, ticket home and a very short note, well, more of a sentence, really: 'We will talk when you get back, H'. I ordered an omelette from room service and a bottle of Chablis. I couldn't face the stares in the dining room from the other guests, or, for that matter, Miss Smug Knickers on reception, so I stayed in our room, now just my room, until morning.

I managed to get an earlier flight than planned and was home by early evening. Howard was waiting in the kitchen and handed me a glass of wine, but no other greeting was forthcoming. As I started to speak, he put his hand up to stop me.

"Firstly, I want to apologise. Leaving you in Paris by yourself was unforgivable, I'm truly sorry for that. And I have been worried about you, of course. I'm glad you're back safely." I opened my mouth to speak but the hand came up again.

"However, this weekend has made me realise what I think we both already knew but weren't facing. Living together has been mostly great, but we hadn't really spent any extended time together due to our crazy work schedules until these recent holidays. When we have had time off work, we want very different things from life. You are a party animal, and I am about as far from that as you can get. You like the finest money can buy, I'm happy with a beer, a curry, and a night in front of the telly. Your description of me as a middle-aged bore was fairly accurate, I suppose, but I'm okay with that. I don't need or want fancy trips abroad, food I don't recognise and wine that costs more than the electricity bill. I want a secure, steady life without drama, and to spend my free time relaxing and seeing places, not fighting with crowds of tourists, in places I'm uncomfortable. We are too different to have a future together, which has made me sad, but I also feel a sense of relief that I can just be me again, and not feel I have to try to live up to your expectations. I can't make you happy without sacrificing so much that makes me happy."

There's not a lot there to disagree with, and at least he didn't say some of the things he could've said, like I am high maintenance, spoilt, selfish, demanding and ungrateful. And so, sadly, Howard and I parted company. Maybe it's time to put on my big girl pants and grow up.

Ian

SWM, GSOH. (In case you don't know, that's single white male, good sense of humour.) One previous owner. Yes, Ian is divorced. Not that it's his fault, of course, Laura just realised things weren't panning out the way she'd hoped, and they wanted different things from life. It happens, who are we to judge?

He's thirty-four, has two kids, Aiden and Becky, and a chocolate Labrador called Billy. He lives in a three-bedroom semi on the new estate near the leisure centre and is self-employed. Not through choice, too much paperwork, really, but needs must. Since he shares custody of the kids, it suits him to organise his own work schedule. It also means Ian paying less child maintenance to Laura, as she can now work full time at Beaverbrook & Bishop, the solicitors on the high street. Which, in turn, also meant the divorce was cheaper. Not that Ian is tight, just financially astute, as he puts it. Ian is like those trainers you keep by the back door. You only keep them to take the rubbish out to the bin when, in truth, they're so scruffy they should be *in* the bin. He isn't exactly that scruffy, just a bit 'got dressed in the dark in a charity shop' looking.

In his defence, the kids are always immaculately

dressed, which is probably down to Laura. They have two nice homes, a purpose-built play area in Ian's back garden (Laura lives in a flat) complete with slide and trampoline, and no expense spared where their needs are concerned. They're not spoilt at all, just well cared for.

Ian, on the other hand, does not waste money on himself. He's very proud of the fact he's had the same car for eight years and mostly gets his clothes from charity shops. He admits to eating food several days after the 'best before' date rather than wasting money throwing it away. He'd never let the kids eat it, of course.

He's pretty laid back, mostly, has been known to throw a few f's at work, but is the perfect dad: patient, thoughtful and makes sure the children are always his priority, no matter what.

So, if your birthday falls on a weekend, or Aiden has chicken pox, or Billy needs a trip to the vet's, or Becky has a ballet exam, you're on your own. Very admirable if you're a parent, impossible to grasp if you're not.

Is Laura the ex-wife from hell? Quite the reverse. She's always reminding Ian he needs to get out more, meet someone new and let his hair down a bit. Not that he has much hair – grade 4 – and his mother does it, which saves some money, job done!

He's of the opinion that once bitten, twice shy. So, he's not overly interested in dating, although he has had a few dates since breaking up with Laura. The problem is, once they discover his situation with the children, they either run for the hills, or worse, want to meet them, move in and be the perfect stepmum. Ian's nowhere near ready for that.

His parents are of the same opinion as Laura, it's high time he moved on, his mother says, plenty more sandwiches in the picnic hamper – try a few and see what you like best is his dad's view. Laura is still a much-loved member of the family, and as she has lost both her own parents, always spends Christmas with Ian, his parents and the children. Ian and Laura are good friends, and it has worked out well. How a new woman in Ian's life would fit in, I'm not sure. Ian's parents and Laura would be fine with it, but the new woman might find it a bit strange.

As a builder, his own home is something of a work in progress. Both children's rooms are amazing, Becky has a dad-made princess bed with pink voile draping from the four poster (courtesy of Laura), and Aiden sleeps in his red spaceship, also made by his dad, complete with control panel, which is really a dimmer switch for his light.

Ian's room, however, is not somewhere you'd want to spend a night. Most of the slats on the bed are broken, so it dips precariously to one side, the walls are a hideous sludgy greeny-brown colour, and the curtains are his nan's old purple flowery ones, circa 1972. His few clothes are just thrown over an old broken kitchen chair and there is no lampshade, just a naked bulb hanging crookedly from the ceiling. I imagine there are a few coffee cups, too, growing something nasty in the bottom like some sort of biology experiment. Laura has offered to decorate it for him many times, but Ian declines. He wouldn't spend any money on anything that wasn't for the children and can't see the need to do anything to fix up his bedroom, as he is the only person to spend time in there.

So, what would attract you to Ian? He's a great dad, he's not afraid of hard work and is an all-round nice chap, if a little frugal. Laura still tells the story of their wedding anniversary when he brought home a miniature pink rose in a pot with a card that read 'Happy Birthday to the best Nana in the world. Love Jamie xxx'. Ian's version of events is that he had ordered a bouquet to collect on the way home, but the florist was taken ill and was unable to fulfil his request. He was given it free of charge by way of an apology. Me? I think he had forgotten to get her anything, and the florist was closed, so he pinched it from the cemetery on his way home. When it was her birthday, he always remembered it, but had no idea of what she might like. Poor woman got a new ironing board one year. I think he means well, just a bit of retraining required.

What do you think?

Jack

Jack is a runner. He runs every single day, rain or shine, sleet or snow, in England, in Germany, in the US, or wherever he happens to be in the world. Personally, I don't get it, I'll only run in an emergency, like I'm about to miss my flight, or the off licence is closing and I'm out of Prosecco. Those are worthy causes. Running for the sake of it I will never understand. It hurts your feet, especially in stilettos, it makes you breathless and it's not a good look, generally. Not that Jack runs in heels, obviously. Jack is obviously your trainers, but not cheap or scruffy like Ian. Jack is very expensive proper running shoes, probably costing at least twice what I'd spend on Prosecco in a month. They're not showy or flash, they are for wearing to get the job done.

I mean, yes, we all need to get some exercise to stay fit and healthy, of course, but what's wrong with Pilates and a bracing walk along the seafront? Or shopping? I mean, it's got to be good for you to carry all those bags of new shoes and clothes up to level four in the car park because the lift in the multistorey is out of order again. If I must exercise, it's a no-brainer.

Apart from this weird obsession, Jack is a normal guy.

He works mostly in the city, the rest of the time he's rushing around the world to God knows where, to meetings with God knows who about God knows what. Clearly, I have no idea of Jack's chosen path, only that he dresses like a Hugo Boss shop mannequin and spends a lot, I mean a lot, of money on his clothes. Even his running shorts cost the equivalent of a meal for two in a very upmarket restaurant. He is quite well respected in his area of expertise, I'm told.

We met at the dentist's; funnily enough, Jack does not have great teeth. Not black and sparsely populated but just not lovely, so clearly not for me. I've seen him quite regularly in Starbucks, too, he's a bit of a coffee addict, apparently. He's always got time to have a chat and has the best sense of humour I've come across in a man. Maybe he just gets my humour (not everyone does) or maybe he's just humouring me (see what I mean?) but whenever we do meet up, we laugh uncontrollably about silly things that other people seem puzzled by. A sense of the ridiculous I believe it's called. He does take turns to pay in Starbucks, so he's certainly not old-fashioned in that respect.

In other ways, he has some antiquated views. His mother was a housewife, and he doesn't see anything wrong with women staying home if the husband is earning enough to keep things ticking over. I tried explaining to him on one occasion that women may enjoy going to work, having some independence, but it was like talking to a wall! He just can't get it. Why would any woman go to work if it's not necessary? I mean, it's not always about finances, I think it's a personal choice. A feeling of self-worth, personal growth and development, too, but each to their own, I guess.

Although he doesn't currently have a special someone, he's clearly a people person. He adores his family, they live up north somewhere, Newcastle or somewhere, I think. He visits them a lot and speaks about them all with barely disguised hero worship. His dad is a retired police commissioner, and his two sisters are both in the force. His mother is the glue that holds them all together and he has some hilarious tales of his childhood that have me with tears rolling down my face. I like Jack, he's ordinary but special at the same time, if you know what I mean. The sort of person who makes a best friend, you could tell him anything at all and he'd never judge you (unless you're swearing, of course) or share your secrets.

He does have one thing he hates and that's swearing from either sex but particularly women. I was once having a rant about my boss, and my language was perhaps a little colourful and I thought he was going to throw up, he looked like I'd punched him right where it hurts. He was so shocked, which I admit I found hilarious! I was having the week from hell at work but that's a poor excuse, I know.

He's very up on current affairs, has opinions on everything from the political situation in Belarus to how teenagers wear their jeans hanging off their bum, but not in an opinionated way, he just says what he thinks without any polish. He'd probably make a great politician; he's fair and honest and really does listen to people.

Having said that, when a neighbour reversed into his Mercedes, after a brief period of calm, until he realised the neighbour had been drinking, the lid came off. Not a single swear word left his lips, but he has a talent for quietly spoken fury. I would have not liked to have been on the receiving end of that, I can tell you. If he's annoyed, he's very annoyed, but again, how can you not respect someone who tells it like it is? There is no agenda with Jack, he is who he is and I, for one, find that quite refreshing.

Kenny

enny must have been born in the 1980s because his style is reminiscent of a line dancer. Seriously, his clothes, hairstyle and taste in music are, to be polite, different. I mean, who wears a cowboy hat? Yep, Kenny does. He's not unattractive, in a very dated way, but the plaid shirts and cowboy boots – really? I didn't even know you could still get them. That's untrue, Kenny is *my* cowboy boots, which I bought many years ago. They live at the back of the wardrobe in a dark corner, so no one sees them. I would honestly love to wear them but I'm conscious of my reputation as the shoe queen being in tatters if I did. Could we keep this embarrassing fact between ourselves please?

Kenny's favourite music is obviously country, too. I'm not sure if he's joking when he says the best thing to come out of the 1980s was him. In his defence, he is from the US, Austin, Texas, as he is fond of telling anyone and everyone, and splits his time between the UK and there.

His dad is a musician. Rumour has it he has worked with some big bands back in the day, or so Kenny would have us believe. I know his father has never been much of a presence in Kenny's life. He also hails from Texas and seems to predominately live there. Kenny's mother, who is British and a little strange, in my humble opinion, was probably the biggest Princess Diana fan ever. There are framed pictures of her all over the house, almost as if she were a family member. She modelled herself on her, too, to the point of obsession, really. For those old enough to remember Princess Diana, Kenny's mother has the same hairstyle, the same way of tilting her head down and looking up at you through her eyelashes with a half-smile. She wears clothes very similar to Princess Diana, which I'm sure were on trend then, but she looks like she's stuck in the eighties, too. She must have studied Diana for years to have perfected it the way she has.

Kenny also has an older sister, Frances, who is also a musician and singer and, in my opinion, the biggest talent in the family. Frankie, as she is known, lives in the UK full time, and having very strong political views, says she has no plans to return to the US any time soon, but we won't go into that.

Back to Kenny, who is worth getting to know, I think. For one, I love the accent and could listen to him for hours. He makes me laugh when he says, "I love your British accent."

I point out that we don't have an accent, he does. "Kenny, you speak English with an American accent. I don't speak American with a British accent!" I say, laughing. Spending time with Kenny is always fun; he has endless anecdotes about his crazy life and fascinating stories about the famous people he's met on his travels.

He's great company, and has impeccable manners, even if he has some antiquated views. He will open the door for you, pull out a chair for you, insist on paying and, whether you find it endearing or irritating, will call you 'ma'am', even though he clearly knows your name.

Kenny is a bit of a dreamer. He talks the talk about where he's going to be ten years from now, when he hits the big time. He's been telling that one for at least eleven years. He's not a particularly great guitarist, certainly no Clapton, but he can play. He can sing, too, but although his voice is good, it's not sensational. His band play regularly in some of the local pubs and clubs and have some loyal followers, but I don't think they have what it takes to get noticed by the record labels. Occasionally, Frankie will sing with them, and her voice is incredible, the audience goes wild when she joins the band, but she has no desire to do it on a permanent basis, just for fun when she's in the mood.

So, what does Kenny have to appeal to you? He is certainly easy on the eye for a start. He is tall, about 6'4"and well-proportioned. I think he has something of Brad Pitt about him, and twinkly eyes that always seem to be on the verge of laughing. Apart from the dress sense, if you're okay with a man who opens doors for you and insists on paying when you go on a date, maybe he's worth getting to know. He's a good listener, always interested in your opinions and good company, too. He is, as I said, in the US probably fifty percent of the time, so you wouldn't be able to count on him being around for special events. He does have a job that allows him the flexibility to work wherever he is – I'm not sure what he does exactly but it's something to do with one of the big supermarkets – and, although he seems to be financially sound, he's ready to 'quit in a heartbeat' when he gets signed up by one of the major record companies. He's just waiting to hit the big time, remember. This job is only temporary, he'll tell you, although he's been doing it for ten years.

If you like music, and don't suffer from second-hand embarrassment, give him a spin.

Luke

L uke, aged approximately four hours, was left on the steps of St Augustine Convent in the coldest February there had been for years. I kid you not, he really was. In one of those plastic folding crates I use for recycling wine bottles, with a filthy blanket his only protection from the cold night.

No one ever found out how he came to be there, or his parentage, but the local gossips (namely me and Katie Bradbury) decided he might be the secret child of Emily Campbell-Watson, who had mysteriously disappeared just before GCSEs and resurfaced about six months later. Of course, Kate and I were just kids at the time, so it's all circumstantial, us mostly basing our theory on two things. Firstly, we seriously disliked Emily Campbell-Watson and her snooty family, and two, Luke bears an uncanny resemblance to Emily's brother Simon, who obviously did not have a baby at the age of fifteen, or ever, if you want to be pedantic.

To be fair, Simon could have been Luke's father, with goodness knows who as the mother, but we wouldn't let that stand in the way of a good story. So, we surmised that, rather than heap shame and embarrassment on the family,

Emily had kept the pregnancy hidden, given birth alone in her bedroom, then put the baby into a crate and crept out to the convent in the dead of night, leaving him to potentially perish in the sub-zero temperatures. It has been said that I have an over-active imagination.

The only concrete truth so far is that Luke really was that baby. He was allegedly found by one of the nuns from the convent, sister Margarita, on her way back from her charity work in Hinkerton. I love a margarita, or a cosmopolitan, but that's a different story and I can't remember the end. Anyway, Luke knew nothing of this until his sixteenth birthday, when his adoptive mother decided to show him all the newspaper cuttings she had kept from the time. Poor Luke, what a birthday, first finding out he was adopted, and then that he had been abandoned as a baby by his birth mother. I believe he doesn't have much of a relationship with his adoptive parents these days, or anyone else, really.

However, he's turned into a fine specimen, if you ask me: wild curly hair, eyes of melted chocolate and a beautiful smile with perfect teeth, and as we know, I have a thing about nice teeth. What my dad would have called a proper bloke, too, he likes tinkering with cars, watching the rugby and he drinks Guinness. Having said that, he's certainly not short on female attention and can talk about any topic you can think of from the benefits of eyebrow waxing to his opinion on styles of wedding dress. Don't try asking him about himself, though. "Oh, you know, not much to tell really," he'll say. No, Luke, we don't know, but we'd love to.

Some of what we do know comes from Samantha Riley, who dated Luke for about a year during college. Luke broke up with her as he needed to concentrate more on his studies and she was suitably devastated – still is, I think.

Luke is a painter, not as in painter and decorator but a real proper painter, as in actual artist. I'm not sure what sort of painter, as I'm not up on modern art, but he has had exhibitions locally and seems to make a reasonable living at it. To be honest, I can't even tell you which way up they're supposed to go, they're all a bit weird, if you ask me. One I saw had what looked like an eye in the middle of a dead flower with horns and slices of pizza at the top. It was called 'Tomorrow', apparently. There was another one that looked to me like a butterfly giving birth to a hedgehog. I wonder what a psychiatrist would make of it.

To me, Luke is my black biker-style boots; they're comfortable, go with just about everything, and are my go-to when I can't decide what to wear. Maybe not the height of fashion but I've always preferred to go my own way with my shoe and boot choices. Like the man I've paired them with, they're not flashy or loud, just quietly there, blending in. Apart from his slightly 'serial killer' artwork, Luke comes across as a nice guy, adaptable and presentable. Smiley, and sort of gentle in his demeanour. I like him.

Matt

I'm not sure whether Matt is for real sometimes. I mean, how many people do you know that are so happy all the time? He's not on drugs that I'm aware of, nor does he appear to have any mental health issues, but he has this permanent grin plastered across his face, which although quite endearing, can make him look a little weird at times. Matt is an estate agent, so perhaps it was part of his training that he must look delighted about everything, even a one-bedroom flat with a mouldy bathroom in the grottiest neighbourhood. Rather than a glass half full person, Matt is more of a glass overspilling. He reminds me of my orange suede shoes: they're a bit of a one-off, I must have bought them to go with something but I've no idea what. They are nice shoes, but a little lively colour-wise. I'm not sure they're really my thing.

Let's not judge him, estate agents can be normal people. What counts as normal I'm not sure, but anyhow I like Matt. I first met him when I sold my flat and was looking for something bigger. He arranged a viewing for me at a very nice house at the end of Queen Street. It was not really what I had in mind, but he insisted it was perfect for me, and I just had to see it. It wasn't at all what I'd told him

I was after, garden too big, bathroom too small, kitchen nearly as old as me, but Matt almost dragged me around, waxing lyrical about everything, practically dancing with excitement. I wouldn't say I'm easily led – in fact, I'm told I can be a tad single-minded – but I somehow found myself telling Matt it was perfect for me and made an offer on the spot. To be fair, I did grow to love it, but it took a while, and I was a little annoyed that I'd allowed myself to catch Matt's enthusiasm.

Matt's family originated in Staffordshire, but I think his dad was in the forces, so they ended up moving all over the place, finishing up in a ghastly 1950s bungalow just outside Oxford. He visits his parents as often as he can, and his married sister who has two children, which makes him a good family-orientated man in my book. Any man who spends time with his mother or sister seems like good husband material to me.

His exuberance is infectious, which in the right circumstance is great; he's always up for playing the fool at parties, quite happy to be the butt of any joke or prank and never loses that silly grin. If any one of his friends or workmates is feeling a little flat, he's very good at cheering them up. Thoughtful, too. When someone leaves the office for pastures new, he is always the organiser of flowers, gifts and a card. However, I do wonder what he would be like if someone was really upset, like if their cat got run over by a bus! In my experience, sometimes it's better to let someone have time to be upset, rather than always try and jolly them out of it.

He does have one very annoying habit, though, which, quite frankly drives me nuts. He has never, to my knowledge, been on time for anything in his life. When I viewed my house, he arrived, somewhat breathless, around 4.25pm for our 4pm appointment. Now maybe this is more about me, but I don't do late, and I have little or no patience with anyone who does. And in this day and age, with mobile phones, etc., how hard is it to call or text to say you've been delayed? I mean, it's just good manners, isn't it? Imagine you're dating Matt, and you're left standing outside the cinema/restaurant/show in the pouring rain for half an hour, feeling like a lemon, how long do you wait before you give up? Or worse, you turn up to marry him at 2pm and he's a no show until half an hour later, by which time you've imagined every scenario from him getting shot by intruders, crushed by a tractor on the A36, or eloping with Sharon with the breast implants and Botox from the Rose and Crown. So… you still think he's worth a chance? Don't say I didn't warn you, just keep a brolly and a good book with you for all that time waiting.

Matt and me

Well, Matt and I were briefly an item. A few days after I bought the house, Matt had called round with a beautiful bouquet of flowers and a decent bottle of champagne. Having had good manners drummed into me by my mother, of course I invited him in, and we opened the bubbles. I had been there less than a week, so was still a little disorganised, but gave him a tour of how things were looking so far. I also found myself showing him my design ideas for the bathroom and kitchen. As per, Matt raved about all my ideas with the enthusiasm of a four-year-old on Christmas morning. Again, I found myself caught up with his excitement and, before I knew it, we'd arranged a date for Thursday evening, under the guise of recommending quality contractors to help me with my plans.

As it turned out, Matt had purchased a slightly run-down Victorian semi the previous year, and he had completely refurbished it, so he does know his stuff and was helpful and knowledgeable in equal measure. He is also great company, with some hilarious anecdotes to tell about some of his experiences as an estate agent. Once, he was showing a house to a young couple with a baby when, after ringing the doorbell to ensure the soon-to-be-divorced owners were at work, let himself and the potential purchasers in. It was going well, until he opened the door to the master bedroom. The husband was in bed with the reason for the divorce. Matt said that, although it was one of the most embarrassing situations he'd ever encountered, it was also one of the funniest. The young couple said they would not be buying the property, as once you've seen that, you can't unsee it, and they would not be able to go in that bedroom without remembering it.

I love to laugh, and my brief relationship with Matt involved a lot of laughter. He was, and is, fun with a capital

F. He is also frequently late with a capital L, which as I said, is a real bugbear of mine. No matter how often I picked him up on it, he would smile that silly grin that was infectious, apologise profusely and I'd temporarily forgive him.

Until, that is, the night I did not get to see Millie and the Macs live at the Apollo. I had been given the tickets by my boss Kevin, who gets freebies for all the best bands. Knowing I was a massive fan, bless him, he gave me tickets and a pass for the after-show party. Not really a party, I knew from previous experience, just a fifteen-minute meet and greet thing with a glass of warm, cheap white wine, a couple of stale sausage rolls and a curly sandwich.

I managed to finish work on time – again, good old Kevin – rushed home and put on my favourite red dress and killer heels and styled my hair in a messy bun. Matt was due to pick me up at 6.30pm, so I was ready by ten past, pacing up and down, looking out of the window at eight second intervals. By 6.29pm, I was starting to panic, knowing Matt's history. 6.31pm I made the first of eleven calls to Matt's mobile, none of which were answered. Trying not to panic, and failing, I called a taxi.

"Best I can do, love, is 7.45, there's a big concert on at the Apollo tonight and we're stretched to the max." After four more attempts with other firms, I was frantic. Desperate measures were called for; I'd have to find a bus. The last time I'd caught a bus, I was around thirteen, so this was not going to be easy. It turned out, there were no bus stops anywhere to be seen as I strutted along in my ridiculous shoes. Google Maps informed me it was a fifteen-minute walk to the Apollo, but Google Maps wasn't wearing four-inch heels. Nor had they mentioned the rain. By the time I reached the Apollo, soaked to the skin, it was 7.40pm. Mr Jobsworth happened to be outside the firmly closed door with that look, you know, arms folded across his chest, pursed lips and the one raised eyebrow.

"'Fraid not, love, entry closed at 7.30 sharp. If I let you in, I'd be breaking the rules, and I can't do that. Should've worn sensible shoes, might have got here on time." Laughing at his own joke, I was sorely tempted to remove said shoes and let him wear one on each ear. No matter what I tried, there was no way in. I was almost in tears when my phone rang. Matt, of course. Within a minute, he'd pulled up outside and leant over to open the passenger door. I decided not to kill him there and then, as that would have jeopardised my safety. Instead, I demanded to be taken home immediately. Matt apologised several times, telling me his last viewing had overrun, and he couldn't call or text as he was with the client. I remained tight-lipped until we got indoors.

I exhaled loudly, before asking the obvious question. "Why did it overrun, Matt? Was it, by any chance, due to the fact you were late to meet the client?"

He had the grace to blush and look down at his shoes. "Look, I understand you're disappointed. I am sorry, I'll make it up to you. I'll get tickets for us to see Chrissy Blackwell; it'll be even better than Millie and the Macs."

"For a start, I've never heard of Chrissy Blackwell, so

that's not any consolation. And secondly, I'm a little more than disappointed. Devastated, drowned and done with your appalling lack of respect. You knew how excited I was but couldn't organise your day to make sure I got there in time. It's bad enough sitting in a restaurant or bar on my own waiting for half an hour for you, or missing the first twenty minutes of a film at the cinema, but this? This is inexcusable, we're done, Matt, please leave." There may have been a few expletives in there too, if I'm honest.

Matt left, I drank several large glasses of Merlot and cried. I still haven't got to see Millie and the Macs.

Nick

I'm not sure Nick is for you, or anyone, for that matter. Don't get me wrong, he's a nice guy. He's just a little strange. Stranger than your average strange, if you follow. And Boring; yes, that's Boring with a capital B. He is like a pair of lace-up ankle boots in a dirty mustard colour with blue tongues. Not like Nick has a blue tongue, obviously, he's not that strange. I'm not explaining this well, I don't think. Nick is like the boots in the charity shop window, which you see and think to yourself, *I can see why someone didn't want them, but who would have bought them in the first place?*

So, he lived with his widowed mother (his dad was killed in a road accident when he was quite young) until she died of cancer a few years ago. Since her death, Nick has remained in the house. Makes sense, really, as the only child, but he hasn't changed anything inside, so it feels a bit creepy. I mean, it's quite dated, net curtains at the windows, his mother's room untouched, her clothes still in the wardrobe as if she's just nipped out to the Co-op for a loaf of bread.

Personally, I find it all a bit weird, and I'm not surprised there is no girlfriend. I wouldn't want to spend a night there, would you? There had been girlfriends before his mother's passing, but I don't think there have been since.

It's hard to guess Nick's age. He's quite young looking, and presentable enough, but has a world-weary look about him that ages him a bit. He also dresses as though his mother bought his clothes, which she possibly did, and he hasn't got around to buying anything new in a few years. Not that he's particularly old-fashioned, but he's hardly a trendsetter, either. He drives a small blue Ford Fiesta, which he's had for years, and works in the accounts department at Palmer and James on the industrial estate near Burger King. I'm not sure what he does, exactly, but it's something fairly unexciting, I think. He leaves the house around 8.20am every weekday and gets back a little before 6pm. He takes a packed lunch to work, too. Sorry, I'm probably being unkind, but I reckon he's carrying on where his mother left off. I'm sure he's perfect for someone, but it certainly is not me.

He has a routine that he sticks to religiously at weekends. On a Saturday morning between 9.30 and 10.30, he goes to the supermarket grocery shopping, takes it home and puts it all away before walking into town, buying a magazine about fishing and getting a coffee at The Coffee Pot. He spends around an hour there, reading his magazine, before taking the long way home along the canal towpath. When he gets home, he hangs his washing out in the garden if it's a nice day, five shirts, several T-shirts, a few pairs of jeans, underwear and socks, all paired up, obviously. If it's raining or cold, I imagine he hangs it all neatly on a clothes airer to dry.

Saturday afternoons, he occasionally goes to watch the football with Mike Turnbull, his colleague/friend from work. They go to the Rose and Crown afterwards for a couple of beers and then onto the Indian on Cresswell Street for a chicken jalfrezi. That's probably inaccurate, Nick isn't adventurous enough to have a jalfrezi, I expect he has a korma.

If you are considering dating Nick and haven't fallen asleep reading about his unexciting life, just wait until you hear about Sundays!

On a Sunday, Nick goes to the newsagent's around 9am, not one for a lie-in, clearly. Then he returns home, spends an hour reading the paper before ironing his shirts for the following week. He then spends a couple of hours batch cooking his meals for the week and putting them into labelled containers ready for freezing when cooled. After that, he heads down to the petrol station to fill up with fuel ready for the working week, uses the car wash and returns home.

About 6.30pm, his cousin Barry arrives, and they go off to the snooker club for some food before playing snooker until 10pm. Nick usually has the steak and mushroom pie with mashed potato and peas, occasionally he has lasagne. A creature of habit.

If you are considering chancing your luck with Nick, you'll need to get past Mel first. Mel is a quiet, mousey blonde girl who works in the newsagent's. She has fancied him for years, spending hours daydreaming about marrying Nick and living happily ever after in his little semi, with a cat called Bo. She obviously has no idea he has a cat allergy.

Oliver

Oliver is possibly – no, probably; no, definitely – the best-looking man in the world… ever. Bar none. There. I've said it.

A few years ago, I was walking home from the Chinese takeaway with my chicken chow mein and sweet and sour pork (Hong Kong style) and I saw Oliver standing outside the Crown, pint in hand, chatting to a few of his friends. To be honest, there aren't many things that can distract me from my Chinese, but I saw Oliver and BANG! Straight into a stupid lamppost headfirst, banged my head and, in the confusion, fell off the side of my shoe, resulting in the most excruciatingly embarrassing five minutes of my entire life (apart from the time my skirt was tucked into my knickers at the office Christmas party, which, to be fair, was almost on a par).

So, there I am, on my knees in the gutter, chow mein strewn across the pavement, ripped tights, grazed shin and seriously dented pride. Uproarious laughter coming from all the guys outside the pub, except Oliver and Andy Taylor, who both rushed over to me, looking very concerned.

"Are you okay?" It's at that moment, I realise Oliver is seriously gorgeous but somewhat lacking in intelligence.

Am I okay? What is he thinking? I'm clearly less okay than I have ever been in my life. I have made a complete spectacle of myself, my ego is so bruised it's practically broken and I have lost £15 worth of dinner (I didn't think it was appropriate to scrape it all off the pavement and put it back in the bag in front of them).

I assure them I'm fine, apart from the heel hanging off my brand new £150-in-the-sale strappy sandals, and with as much decorum as I could muster, got back on my feet – well, foot – and limped off, tears threatening to pour from my eyes at any second. As if I hadn't suffered enough embarrassment at the time, Oliver the bloody hero knocked on my door an hour and a half later to see how I was! Really! By this time, of course, I've had a shower, have no make-up on, my hair is wet and hanging like rats' tails and I'm wearing my favourite Minnie Mouse PJs that are a size twelve (and I am not!) and my Teletubby slippers my mother bought me for a joke. Oh, fantastic! This may go down as the worst day of my life. I mean, how likely is Oliver to ask me on a date now? Honestly, I've got more chance of marrying Simon Cowell and having triplets. Please don't misunderstand that comment, I have absolutely no desire to marry Simon Cowell, I'm just stating the unlikeliness.

Anyway, at least Oliver has a good sense of humour. Every time I've seen him since then, he waves and says, "Chow!" and roars with laughter. At least he knows who I am, I suppose.

Oliver is my favourite shoes, obviously. They are sage-green suede sort of mules, with a lattice pattern cut into them and a tiny gold edging strip. They are so gorgeous I never wear them. I'd hate to ruin them and, if I'm honest, they are a teeny-weeny bit small for me. But, I like to visualise myself in them with my gold wedding dress when I'm a real size eight and my feet have shrunk. I also visualise Oliver as the groom but now I'm being delusional, so I'll stop.

So, what else can I tell you about him? About 6'2" or thereabouts, very dark hair, almost black, with the most stunning blue, piercing, twinkling, smiling eyes. I may have mentioned he's not hideously ugly, either. He has a flat overlooking the marina, but he's not around much. He does something secret, I think, possibly forces or government related, as he never discusses his work, ever, with anyone. His friends always say he is a bodyguard for HRH someone but who knows! He goes away for long periods at a time, is super fit, and I can't think of a bad thing to say about him, other than he's not dating me, which is a bit silly of him, in my opinion.

There was a long-term relationship with some stunningly attractive, size eight, lovely girl called Melissa who all of us girls tried our best to hate. Not an option, she was such a sweet girl on the few occasions she came out locally. He never spoke about her after she stopped staying with him, so we have no idea what happened, but he's definitely single.

Oliver is also quite sporty – rugby, tennis, swimming – and is outstanding at them all. He's not a fanatic, by any means, but does like to keep in shape and it shows. He's competitive without being over the top; the sort of person you would want on your team. He is almost too good to be true, I honestly can't think of anything I don't like about him. Apart from him seeing me in my Minnie Mouse PJs, obviously, but that's not really his fault.

There have been a few women breezing in and out of Oliver's life. Almost all of them tall, slim, with long flowing locks, dazzling white teeth and a personality to match. Sickening but reinforcing the point I'm clearly not his type. I am not tall, possibly a size eight if you were to slice me in half, and my hair resembles a Brillo pad that has been electrocuted. My teeth are all right, but I wouldn't get a role in a toothpaste advert. One of Oliver's girlfriends, Mercedes (what were her parents thinking?), was around for quite a while but rumour has it she dumped him for some aspiring footballer who played for Accrington Stanley.

I have this recurring dream that Oliver approaches me in the street when I've just left the hairdresser's looking like Jennifer Aniston and asks to have a drink with me. We end up in a fabulous upmarket restaurant eating crayfish linguine and drinking Chablis while Oliver tells me I'm the only woman he's ever felt comfortable with, I'm just perfect in every way and he's been secretly in love with me for years. Then I wake up feeling nauseous; I didn't like to tell him I'm allergic to crayfish.

So, if you are tall, slim and gorgeous, and he sounds like your type, pop into the Crown one Thursday evening and see how it goes. Just don't expect me to be your friend!

Paolo

Paolo has the sort of hair you want to run your fingers through. Actually, it usually looks like someone already has. Not scruffy, exactly, just sort of tousled. He's very casual in every way, clothes, opinions, attitude. I can't imagine him getting hot under the collar about anything to be honest, he's just so laid back that nothing seems to bother him. I mean, even when something terrible happens and it's all over the news, he just says, "Yeah, that's not good, is it?" as if he were chatting about the exchange rate of the euro. For me, he's a pair of expensive leather flip-flops in a nice shade of chocolate brown. Not too fancy but look good (provided you've had a pedicure) and versatile. The sort of thing you throw on in a hurry that will go with most things if you're only nipping to the takeaway. No big deal kind of footwear that kind of matches his laid-back vibe.

Maybe that's why he's single, he doesn't seem to be able to muster enthusiasm for anything, never mind a girlfriend. Maybe he's lazy. I mean, it really seems like conversation is too much effort when he's out. He is always clean and presentable but in a non-ironed way, if you know what I mean. He just sits in the pub with a few friends, occasionally nodding his agreement or pulling that 'yeah, whatever you guys think is fine with me' kind of expression. Even his smile, which happens often, is like a half smile, as though he's not that amused or can't be bothered to use all the muscles required for a beaming grin. Maybe his friends are not terribly interesting, or maybe that's just Paolo.

Imagine you're his girlfriend for a minute, you've spent hours getting ready for his office Christmas party, hair straightened within an inch of its life, perfect make-up and a stunning super sexy dress and killer heels. You feel a million dollars as you sashay out the door to greet him. "Ta-dah! How do I look, Paolo?"

"Yeah, nice," is the lacklustre response! Nice? Who the hell wants to look nice? "Wow, stunning, gorgeous," or anything but nice.

Okay, so he doesn't have an office Christmas party because he doesn't work in an office, but you get my drift, right? He is a self-employed kind of alternative nutritional therapist. I don't really know exactly what he does but it's all related to self-healing and stuff. Apparently, he can tell if you're gluten intolerant by waving sticks over your head and 'asking the universe', according to Christie McWhatsit from our book club. Personally, I think she goes to him because he's cute and good looking, but she swears by his alternative methods; he apparently cured her IBS by recommending she eats every two hours and takes some hideous looking pills made from crushed chrysanthemum roots and alligator urine or something! Well okay, maybe

I made that up but it's something weird. Interesting that Christie comes up with a different ailment every other week; an excuse to see Paolo, obviously. She must be minted, though; I think it's £100 per consultation plus the cost of whatever disgusting remedies he recommends. I've seen him at that new vegan café type place in town, so he's probably one of them, too; not that I have anything against vegans, obviously, but I'm defo a bacon sarnie kind of girl. All that beetroot, avocado and watermelon smoothie type stuff just doesn't float my boat. I mean, slimming clubs really need people like me, I see it as helping the economy by eating pizza and cake (not at the same time, of course). Plus, I spend a fortune on indigestion remedies and 'get thin quick' underwear, so I really feel I'm doing my bit.

His consulting room is very nice, apparently, all pale sage-green and creams, with huge cushions and crystals everywhere. He is rumoured to be a hypnotherapist too, but I'm not sure about that. Imagine what you might tell him while under hypnosis, you'd never live it down! Mind you, lying on the couch while Paolo talks to you in a soothing voice, with spa music playing softly in the background… I'm giving that some serious consideration. If only he did massage!

Did I mention his hands? OMG, he has the most beautiful hands for a man. I mean, not feminine at all, not too manly, just slim fingers, nails short but not bitten or scruffy, just perfect. Personally, I couldn't go out with someone who bites their nails but we're all different, aren't we?

So, if you think Paolo might be your cup of rosemary, mint and ginger tea, why not book in with some mystery ailment and see what happens? Good luck!

Quentin

Okay, so Quentin was previously a window cleaner/ handyman called Barry but, after getting a taste for amateur dramatics, he became someone so far removed from Barry, he's unrecognisable. When he was Barry, he could have been like a pair of loafers but as Quentin, for me, he's more something that isn't quite what you would expect: purple patent brogues or something of that nature.

It all started when his neighbour asked him to help with the scenery he was painting for a production at the community centre to be performed by the AAA. Nothing to do with cars or alcohol, the group call themselves the Amateur Actors Association, which is self-explanatory.

It was some Agatha Christie type play, not sure of the storyline other than several grisly murders, but there was a butler in it called Watkins who, on the third night of a seven-night run, fell off the stage carrying a tray of pretend sherry and broke his ankle. Poor bloke, the audience thought it was part of the play and roared with laughter. Anyway, they had no one to cover the role as Gerry – the understudy's wife, had gone into labour – so Barry offered to help. The part of Arthur Watkins, although on stage a fair bit, only ever said, "Yes, m'lady," or handed round drinks and canapés. The AAA were impressed and asked him if he'd play a slightly bigger part in the next production, namely Norman Ashurst, the murderer's first victim. Apparently, his on-stage death was so brilliantly authentic, he should've won an Oscar!

Barry then progressed to wearing a silk scarf with his jeans and blazer, growing his hair so it just curls and touches his collar and sporting a funny little goatee beard before changing his name to Quentin Le Velle. A few walk-on 'extra' roles followed in little known dramas on Channel 4, before his big break, a four-second appearance as the next-door neighbour in a Honda advert! Bless him, he's no Tom Cruise, but he thinks he has similarities to Benedict Cumberbatch. Can't see it myself.

But who is Quentin/Barry as a person? He is a charming, polite, well-mannered man who loves animals and calls his mother every other day to make sure she's okay. That gives him points from me: any man who cares about his mum will look after his wife, I think. Although his new name and appearance and mannerisms could intimate he's gay, he certainly is not. Not according to the number of women he knew very well in his window cleaning days. Lynn Potts was madly in love with him, and they apparently had a very physical relationship until her husband returned from Dubai, when she saw how much he'd earned while he was away and decided to work things out with him. Not that I'm saying she's like that, but if you had to choose between someone who earns enough to buy a four-bed detached house in one year, or a window cleaner? And she is high maintenance, as they say.

Quentin is also very tactile, not in a pervy touchy way, but he will put his hand on your arm when he's talking to you, which I find quite sweet; he makes you feel like he's really interested in what you have to say. He just comes across as an all-round nice guy. Sorry, there's the nice word again, but it does fit him.

I do know his mother, who is a charming lady, quite frail since having a stroke a few years back, but she is always smiling, with proper twinkly blue eyes like Barry's, I mean Quentin's. And she is so proud of him, telling anyone who stops to chat, "My boy Quentin, he's an actor, you know! I expect you've seen him on the television." Then she'll show the photograph she carries everywhere, the one the *Daily Echo* used when they ran the story, "Local lad loving the limelight in Lowestoft," when he went on tour with some play or other.

Unless he lands a major role, he'll never be rich, so forget him if you're looking for an easy life. He pays for someone to check on his mother twice a day and do any little jobs she can't manage while he's away. He also regularly donates a significant amount to a local charity that supported his sister during her lifetime. She passed away at the age of twenty due to a congenital condition.

I told you he was nice, see? I hope he meets the right girl soon, and I hope she's not called Linda or Lucy. Lucy La Velle sounds like a porn actress to me!

Ross

While all the other lads at school were playing football, Ross was studying. When the other boys started to notice girls, Ross was studying. While the rest of our group was learning what happens when you drink red wine, cider and vodka on the same night, Ross was still studying. So, it goes without saying that while the rest of us were regretting our lost opportunities for getting into uni, Ross was already there.

Ross doesn't look like a geek in any way. In fact, I think he looks more like a film star from back in the day; chiselled good looks, they used to call it. How you might imagine a young Hugh Grant, in my opinion, with a smaller nose. He is tall enough for most girls, at least 6'1", slim with thick, shoulder-length hair in a shade I'd call dirty blond. He has fabulous teeth (you remember I have a strange obsession with teeth), with a kind of lop-sided smile that's quite endearing.

He is a great listener, as my cousin Manda told me after her one and only date with him several years ago in college.

"Hey, Manda. How was your date with gorgeous Ross?"

"Dreamy, he's sooo good looking and perfect boyfriend

material. He listened intently to everything I said, you know, like really listened. He was so interested; I can't wait to see him again."

"So, tell me all about him, what's he studying? How old is he? Where does he live? What are his likes/dislikes/hobbies, etc?"

"Oh… I don't know. I didn't ask him anything…"

Surprisingly, there was no second date. Manda is a gorgeous creature, and I love her dearly, but she is totally self-absorbed. The last time I saw her was a few weeks ago when we met up at the shopping centre for a coffee. After choking back the sobs that my cat had been run over, I had been passed over for a big promotion at work, and someone had hit my car in the car park and not told me (£750 repair bill), she said, "Oh love, never mind. How do you like my new jacket…? Half price in the sale… only £240! It's fabulous, don't you think?" So, Manda is still boyfriend-less and Ross is still available.

I wouldn't say Ross is boring. I mean, who am I to judge? But I don't think he's my type. Ross's idea of a great night is a pasta bake (from Waitrose, to be fair), two cans of cider and a fascinating documentary on architecture in eighteenth-century Kazakhstan on Channel 4. I overheard him telling someone in the bank about how pharaoh ants utilise three types of pheromones. I had no idea what he was talking about, so I went home and googled them! It took me a few minutes to realise I was turning into someone I didn't recognise. However, if you're doing a degree in the history of the wheelie bin and need some help, Ross is probably the person to call upon.

Ross has an identical twin brother, Stuart, if you like the look of him, with a very non-identical personality. He failed most of his exams at school, is not very reliable and has probably never read a book in his life. Too busy having a good time to worry about tomorrow, or how he'll pay the rent. He's fun to be around, always up for an adventure but always penniless and happy for you to foot the bill.

Also a plus, in my humble opinion, is Ross is not into sport on any level. Doesn't watch it, doesn't play it and has no competitive streak. Not only would you escape the usual football post-mortem on a Saturday evening, but you can also beat him at Monopoly and he won't care. I wouldn't recommend taking him on at Trivial Pursuit, though, you have a 0% chance of winning and no one likes a smart-arse, do they?

If Ross were a pair of shoes, he would be a pair of charcoal-grey trainers, not really cheap but not overpriced either. Just average, boring trainers. Personally, trainers are not on my list of things I need in my life. I would only be seen in them if I were going to the gym. And, as you've probably worked out for yourself, if I were in the gym, it would be a ruse to accidentally bump into the gorgeous Oliver. Or maybe if there were a bar with a happy hour or free Prosecco.

So, this is very embarrassing, but I need to come clean. Yes, I did date Ross briefly. Don't get me wrong, I'm not embarrassed about dating Ross – well, maybe a little bit – it was how I came to date him that's my problem. As was the case in my youth, and a few more years, I did love a good night with the girls, which invariably involved alcohol. It was on one of these nights, we ended up at Sam's Bar on karaoke night. And for some inexplicable reason, when I have had a few drinks, I have a tendency to think I'm a cross between Madonna and Agnetha from ABBA. I have even been known to be all the Spice Girls on my own, but that's not the embarrassing bit.

Even though Becky tried to stop me, bless her, I ended up on the stage with the microphone, attempting to belt out 'You're the One That I Want' from the film *Grease*; maybe it was the leggings and black leather jacket that made me think I was Olivia Newton-John. Yes, sometimes my fashion sense is a little off too. Believe it or not, even that isn't the embarrassing bit. That happened when I thought I had clocked Stuart (Ross's twin brother), started singing to him and promptly fell clean off the stage on top of him. In my defence, they are identical, and I had possibly consumed more alcohol than the recommended weekly amount in one evening.

The rest of the evening is a bit of a blur, to be honest, but apparently, Ross – who the whole time I thought was Stuart – made sure I got home without any further mishaps and we arranged to meet up a day later to see some crappy film at the Odeon. On meeting outside, he insisted on buying my ticket, drink and popcorn and we settled in our seats to wait for the film to start. You know, don't you? It was at this point he said, "I can't believe you agreed to go out on a date with me to be honest. Stuart reckons you thought I was him, otherwise you'd never have said yes."

It took less than a nanosecond for my face to recover its composure, and I laughed (well more of a squeak really) and replied, "Wow, your brother is a bit conceited, isn't he? Of course I didn't think you were Stuart, you're much better looking than him!" Oscar nomination coming up, I'm sure. Well, at least he believed me, so how could I then turn down a second date, or third or fourth without looking like a grade-A b--ch?

We dated for a while. What I learned about the Aztecs and the Incas is four hours of my life I'll never get back. Did you know the Aztecs spoke Nahuatl and the Incas spoke Quechua? Thought you'd be impressed! I was wondering how to extricate myself from the situation when Ross casually said over a Waitrose risotto, "You know, I'm not sure this is going anywhere for us, Hannah. I mean, you're a great girl and all that, but you're not really on my wavelength academically or intellectually, no offence. You also behave like a drunk teenager at times, and you laugh like a hyena. It seems to me I see life as an opportunity to grow and learn, but you see life as one long party with getting drunk as one of your hobbies."

Well, that was easy. We agreed to part as friends, ha! How many of your friends do you want to poke in the eye with a pencil? Exactly. I did think about telling him I had thought he was Stuart when I agreed to go out with him, however, while I may be unintellectual and a drunk hyena, I'm not a cow.

Sebastian

I wouldn't say Sebastian has OCD as that would be presumptuous and judgemental of me, but he's certainly unusual in comparison to other men I know. One of my cousins dated Sebastian a couple of years ago. It wasn't a match made in heaven, and it didn't end well (mainly down to my cousin's behaviour!). Seb is a very classy pair of black patent strappy sandals, not stupidly high but enough heel to make them dressy without being over the top.

On the surface, Seb is an ordinary guy, presentable, sociable and, it must be said, very easy on the eye. He is in his thirties, I think, and lives in a very swish apartment overlooking the river. You know the ones, they used to be an old warehouse, old red brick with huge windows and a price to match. The kind of place where the people who live there are either very comfortably off, or up to their armpits in debt, with a mortgage the size of Bristol. I'm not certain which category Seb is in, but he comes across as wealthy but not flashy, if you know what I mean. For those of us who are car snobs, he drives a Mercedes E Class, about two years old, slick and black without personalised plates (thankfully). Having said that, he also cycles, mainly on weekends and evenings, and no, he doesn't wear Lycra, another point in his favour. I also happen to know, courtesy of my gossipy cousin, that he's something of a film buff. So much so that he has a sort of home cinema room in his apartment, which most of the other residents call bedroom two.

He works with his brother. They have several car dealerships in the local area, most notably the Mercedes place just off the motorway by the retail park on the edge of town. Rumour has it that his brother runs the body shop side of the business and Seb is the main man (aka the CEO) of the sales side. Their parents lived in Saudi Arabia until recently but have now moved back to the UK as his dad retired and they now have a beautiful house a few miles outside of town. I haven't been there but Jess (the cousin who dated Seb) gave me a detailed description of both house and parents. Mother is lovely, friendly and bakes wonderful cakes while Dad is a quiet man, spending most of his time tending their beautiful garden or playing golf. The house is stunning, modern but with a comfortable feel, the kind of place you'd take your shoes off at the door, but it would be okay to put your bare feet up on the sofa.

So, back to the main man. Jess and Seb met at the tennis club at the beginning of summer, though what Jess was doing there is beyond me, she's the most un-sporty person I know, after myself, obviously; it's a family trait, I think. She never walks anywhere if a cab is available and the last time she wore a pair of trainers was back in school. My personal opinion is that she had heard Seb frequented the tennis club and was looking for a way in. To be fair, my cousin is stunningly attractive, beautiful auburn hair, cute freckles and a figure most of us would die for. She is also witty, funny and very adept at getting her own way… whatever Jess wants, she invariably gets. Before poor Seb knew what hit him, they were having dinner at Mamma Arianna's, with champagne, obviously. And he was under her spell.

Being Jess has always meant people fall over themselves to win her affection, and our friend Seb was no exception. Within weeks, Jess was spending a lot of time at Seb's and it was apparently going well. What Jess had failed to realise was that, spending her whole life with people adoring her, she has never really done much for herself, or anyone else for that matter. Seb had cooked for her, taken her out to amazing restaurants and generally waited on her hand, foot and finger. Jess, however, had lounged around, waiting for Seb to cook for her, clear up behind her and attend to her every need. Pretty much a one-way street, it seemed. Seb started complaining that his immaculate apartment was messy, Jess was leaving stuff everywhere like she lived there, and she wasn't making much contribution to the relationship. Ha! I have known her for my entire life, tell me something I don't know. (While I love her dearly, my cousin is a lazy, untidy slob who seems to feel it's beneath her to tidy up, clean, cook or do anything remotely helpful. Her own place, although cleaned on a weekly basis by the lovely Maria for £50 a week, is so untidy, I'm surprised Jess can even find two matching shoes to wear in the morning.)

So, the arguments began, Seb asking Jess as politely as possible to tidy her stuff away and at least remember to put things back she had used, mainly his vast collection of films, his pride and joy, stored categorically then alphabetically. His shoe closet was similarly well organised, work shoes, going out shoes, sports shoes all categorised and colour appropriate. In his kitchen, tins were all stored faced up like in Sainsburys and the forks were like army soldiers in the cutlery drawer, all lined up ready for battle. And God help anyone who doesn't fold the tea towel properly and hang it tidily on the oven door handle. Jess, however, is the sort of person who will clip her toenails in the lounge while watching TV, bits of unpleasantness flying around the room, then stroll off to bed without even realising you're about to kill her. The Row, or as Jess calls it, "Seb's final flip over absolutely nothing," happened on a Sunday morning – Easter Sunday, as I recall – when Jess had got chocolate all over the silk bedspread from eating the ridiculously extravagant chocolate egg Seb had given her in bed. She hadn't got him anything, by the way. Anyway, Seb told her she was a thoughtless spoilt child who needed to grow up and take responsibility for her actions, asking her to consider the cost of having the bedspread dry cleaned, along with all the other carnage she had caused in his flat; the red wine stain on the cream rug, the broken shower hose and the stiletto heel marks on the solid oak floor in the hallway. Taking himself off for a shower to cool off, he didn't hear Jess take every single film in his DVD collection, all 2,397 of them, and change the contents of nearly half of them, leaving them in a heap on the floor, before scattering the remains of the Easter egg on the aforementioned cream carpet. I think Jess is still under the illusion she dumped Sebastian, and he's too much of a nice bloke to say otherwise, so we'll leave it there.

Tim

Tim and I lived together for a while after university in a gorgeous Victorian terraced house across the road from the station. When I say lived together, I mean we shared a house, not as a couple but as friends. It was only for about six months but we got to know one another well. Money was tight but we split the bills and groceries down the middle, apart from the alcohol, for which I was solely responsible. As Tim so eloquently put it, my capacity to drink Prosecco puts many a man to shame. Not that Tim doesn't like a drink, it's just not an essential part of his evening, unlike my good self, who opens a bottle of wine before I've even got my coat off most nights! Although I was frequently a bit squiffy, and Tim was frequently sober, we got along well, laughed a lot and had loads in common. I view Tim as my slippers: warm, comfy and always there waiting for me when I got home. When you've had a crappy day, you missed the bus home and then got caught it a monsoon style storm, you just need to put your slippers on (and pour yourself a nice glass of something sparkly, obviously). It was during this time in my life I acquired Cat, as she is affectionately known, courtesy of Tim. Did I tell you Tim is a vet? Anyway, I'd just broken up with the man of the moment, the man of my dreams, who turned out to be the man of my nightmares, but that's another story.

Obviously, Tim loves animals, and they love him, which says a lot about a man, in my opinion. One Sunday morning, in the most torrential rain and winds, Tim nipped up to the veterinary practice to get some medication for our elderly neighbour's dog who was on its last legs, as a little favour as she was such a sweetie (well, they both were, actually). On parking round the back, he found a soggy dilapidated cardboard box, almost fell over it to tell the truth, and nearly left it there, thinking it was just some rubbish someone had left there. Being Tim, who is the only person I know who is as nosey as me, he pulled back a corner and saw inside a very bedraggled kitten, thin and shivering and feeling very sorry for herself. Of course, he put it straight in the car and rushed back to the house, where we dried her off with an old towel and made her a little bed from one of my many baskets. Tim checked her over and believed her to be around twelve weeks old – apparently you can tell by the teeth – although she appeared not to weigh as much as she should and she was certainly very hungry, although Tim laughed out loud when I suggested giving her a tin of tuna. He went back out and got the appropriate food and a little dish for water and food and Cat's new life with us began. As an Audrey Hepburn fan, I considered calling her Holly Golightly, which Tim found ridiculous. He suggested Marmaduke (for a girl? Really?) and after several hours of heated debate, settled on Cat.

In response to Tim's attempts to call her Marmaduke, she did wee on his shoe in the hallway, but apart from that one occasion, settled into our little home beautifully. Until, of course, the Melissa incident.

While Tim would be considered stunningly good looking by many women – and men, probably – he's completely unaware of just how attractive he is, bless him. There was certainly no shortage of admirers, particularly at work, where the vet's practice was inundated with patients brought in by overdressed young (and older) women with fluttering false eyelashes, short skirts and an inappropriate amount of cleavage on display. He seemed perplexed, particularly by Mrs Huntingdon-Smythe, whose horse apparently suffered from toothache, earache and, interestingly, occasional agoraphobia, resulting in Tim getting called out on a regular basis to her home address, often late in the evening when Mr H-S was away on business. Tim seemed oblivious, remarking to me one evening that he found it odd that someone would request an emergency vet at 9pm, wearing very skimpy silk pyjamas in the stables. I mean, it was about eight degrees at the time! As always, Tim found nothing wrong with the horse, deciding that perhaps his owner had some issues of her own.

It was around November when I first heard the name Melissa mentioned. She had attended the vet's practice with a rabbit that had allegedly just appeared in her back garden. She had asked all her neighbours if it belonged to them, even putting a little note in the newsagent's window, but sadly no one came forward to claim it, and she was apparently allergic to rabbit fur due to her asthma, and could not possibly accommodate it. So, we end up with a rabbit we called Roger (yep, Tim chose that one) and the lovely Melissa ended up taking Tim out for dinner as a thank you. With claws like hers, straight into Tim before he even realised, Melissa must have been a cat in a previous life.

Things moved incredibly quickly from then on, with Melissa and Tim's relationship going from nought to sixty in about six weeks. Mel (as I took to calling her as I knew she hated it) became a frequent visitor to our house, criticising every detail of it in her very uncritical way. "However do you two manage in this teeny tiny kitchen? I mean it's cute but sooo small, where on earth do you store everything? And you have no entertaining space, don't you find it a little claustrophobic? And one bathroom? Ugh!"

Tim seemed, as usual, oblivious to her shortcomings, just bewildered that someone as attractive as Melissa could be so besotted with him. He's quite naive, but that's what makes him so adorable. It sounds like I'm not a Mel fan, and to be fair to the girl, I'm not. I accepted her, made her welcome, made myself scarce as and when possible, and really did try to like her. Then… I almost throttled her. She'd called in unannounced one Saturday while Tim was at work, and I was working from home. I hate being interrupted when I'm working, so although I was polite, I wasn't exactly enthused by her presence. The reason for her untimely visit was to drop off a bottle of Sancerre and some pistachio nuts for 'Timmy', as she was going to a girls' night and wanted to leave him something nice, bless her! At this moment, Cat, startled by a passing motorbike, shot across the room, resulting in tripping Melissa up, who managed to break a perfectly manicured nail as she landed half on the coffee table and half on the floor. This resulted in Melissa taking a wild swing at Cat with her foot, catching her on her back leg, which, along with her calling Cat a mangy little fleabag, caused me to react in a manner I'm not overly proud of. In response, Melissa called me a jealous cow, saying I'd tried everything to split them up as I clearly wanted Tim for myself. Did she not realise I'd been living under the same roof as him for six months and neither of us ever even considered that as an option? Tim's like a brother to me. So, the dilemma was now: what to say to Tim?

Well, in the end, I said nothing, of course. Tim ended up with Melissa, and I got Cat and Roger Rabbit. Quite honestly, I'd have had a family of cockroaches rather than Melissa, but it took Tim four years of marriage before he saw the light. Bless him, it's a good job he's on a good salary as the maintenance for the children must cost a packet. He's available and, in my opinion, a great catch. Pop into the vet's with your pet tarantula and see what you think.

Uca

Obviously, Uca is not his real name, but everyone calls him Uca to the point where most people think that is his name. When his sister was small, she couldn't pronounce Luca, so Uca stuck. What made me chuckle was when I met his sister, who is now nineteen, she told me her name was Bella, but that Uca calls her Ella.

Carmelo's is the best Italian restaurant for miles around. Uca is the star that lights up the whole restaurant. His dazzling smile and twinkling eyes seem to make him glow, like he's full of electricity, or he has eaten a light bulb. He has a way of making you feel like you are an old friend who has come to have dinner with him, and he's delighted to see you. There is a sincerity about him, he is genuinely thrilled to see you. I can't think of anywhere better to go for an amazing meal that is as warm and welcoming as Carmelo's. After what happened to their father, it's incredible that they kept going at all, never mind with the commitment and enthusiasm they show.

Uca has been a part of the family business since he was old enough to wash up standing on a stool, as has Bella. He will happily tell you, there was no question of him doing anything else, it's in his blood. I remember his father

Vincenzo with fondness, always a smile and a kind word and asking after the family. Quieter and less ebullient than his son but a warm and kindly man. One Sunday every month, when the restaurant was closed, Vincenzo and Uca would spend the day cooking nutritious meals and serving them at the local homeless shelter, a tradition that Uca and Bella continue to this day, despite what happened to their father.

So, I expect you want to know what happened to Vincenzo. It was only a few years ago, so you may have read about it in the newspapers at the time. Not only did the Carmelo family serve food at the homeless shelter, they also often took any leftover food from the evening down to the bridge, where some homeless people shelter from the elements if the hostel is full, which it always is. One of the men there, not a regular or a man known to any of the others, accused Vincenzo of giving him a smaller serving of food than the others and became quite agitated. The situation escalated with several other people getting involved. The man pulled a knife and threatened another man, so Vincenzo intervened to try to defuse the situation and was stabbed. Despite the ambulance crew and everyone's best efforts, Vincenzo died, and the man was arrested and charged.

Uca and the family were obviously devastated, and it was thought they would close the restaurant down, but seeing the outpouring of love and support from the townsfolk, they reopened a few weeks later with Uca taking his father's place at the helm. To his credit, Uca continues the tradition of helping feed homeless people, saying always it is what his father would want him to do; one bad apple doesn't spoil the whole bunch.

As footwear, I see Uca as my grey suede ankle boots with the studded straps and the merest hint of sparkle. They were more than I would normally spend on one pair of boots, but they make me feel very glamorous when I wear them. A small heel, just enough to elevate them and me, and super stylish. They are also very soft and sexy, just like Uca.

Obviously Uca doesn't have much time for any sort of social life, although there have been several girlfriends over the years. I expect they struggled with the lack of time Uca has to spare while running the business. So, if you're thinking he sounds perfect for you, be mindful – you would have to be accepted by the whole family, as they spend almost every waking hour together. On the plus side, you would get to eat the most delicious food every day and drink Chianti, so that gets my vote. Although, you'd need to forget about watching your weight! All that pasta!

Vern

I have more respect and admiration for Vern than almost anyone on the planet. Having said that, I also question his sanity, to be honest. Vern teaches maths to teenagers at the comprehensive school in the town centre. Who in their right mind chooses to spend every day with a bunch of surly, monosyllabic kids who are glued to social media every waking hour? Vern is a legend, in my opinion; I'd rather poke myself in the eye with a pencil than do that job even for a day. You must be a special kind of person to be a teacher, and Vern is certainly one of a kind.

He tells the story to his friends of how difficult he found school as a child after struggling to achieve for several years, with his teachers telling him he was lazy and lacked focus. One teacher actually told him he would be lucky to get a job stacking fruit in a supermarket with his lack of ability! It turned out he did lack focus, he couldn't see well enough to be able to do the work, and it was a young supply teacher, Miss Matthews, who realised he had a problem with his eyesight. Miss Matthews also wore glasses and had been the only one to take the time to find out why Vern was struggling. She also put in extra time after school to enable Vern to achieve his full potential and Vern says she changed his life. Her support, after the terrible experience he had been through, gave him belief in his ability for the first time and instilled a desire to make a difference to other children's lives.

Vern even looks like a teacher. Well, how I envisage teachers: slightly out of control curly hair, large dark-rimmed glasses, checked shirt not fully tucked in, with a kind of 'I may have got dressed in the dark' look. He reminds me a little of Tigger from *Winnie-the-Pooh*, with a boundless energy and a thirst for knowledge. He also spends more time smiling than almost anyone I know. Vern's mother is Vietnamese, and his father is Jamaican. He's stunningly good looking, I can't even begin to tell you. He also has no idea of this important fact, which makes him even more endearing. There's nothing worse than a man – or woman, for that matter – who knows they're attractive and behaves like they're something special. He reminds me of my fur-lined rust-coloured slouch boots. In fact, they're more of a rich ginger, very old and a little bit the worse for wear, but I have never found another pair of boots in such a scrummy colour, so they're staying until they disintegrate. An absolute favourite of mine, like Vern.

We met at the dentist, which turned an experience I'm usually not a fan of into a great day. I was running late (I know, that is unthinkable for me), and we were both reversing towards the only vacant parking space in the car park. Ready for an argument, I was pleasantly surprised when he gestured for me to take the space. By the time I had parked in a reasonably straight line and recovered my bag from the back seat, he was back, having parked in the street opposite, just in time to see me catch my heel as I got out and face plant the car park, spilling the entire contents of my bag everywhere. Just a normal day for me, really. To Vern's credit, he didn't ask if I was okay – clearly my embarrassment was excruciatingly painful – nor did he laugh. He just casually said, "Well, that's an unusual way to get a man to notice you, which I already had as it happens. After our appointments, could I buy you a coffee and a new pair of tights?" I love a man with a sense of humour, so it was a date of sorts. Me with a big hole in my tights and a fat lip, Vern dribbling coffee all down his shirt as the anaesthetic hadn't fully worn off after his filling.

We exchanged numbers and agreed to meet the following evening at the new Mexican restaurant in the high street. Not only was Vern waiting for me with a glass of Prosecco and some olives (fabulous and disgusting, in that order), but also a beautifully wrapped package. A three-pack of tights, right colour, right size, so I was prepared for my next catastrophe, apparently. I thought, 'This one's a keeper'.

Vern and I dated for a couple of months. I met his friends and family, and he met mine. We had such a great time; Vern is kind, thoughtful and has a great sense of humour. He always sees the best in people, is curious and genuinely interested in others. I expect you're wondering why it didn't last. The truth is, we realised at some point that there wasn't really that spark. We had become such good friends but there was something vital missing from the relationship. We are still close, meeting up once a month for a meal and to catch up, but Vern is more like a brother to me. I look forward to seeing what happens next for him. He deserves someone wonderful.

Will

Will and I met at a charity fundraiser event that I attended with my good friend Tim (remember him? Married the lovely Melissa). In fairness to Will, I was looking rather fabulous that evening, if I do say so myself.

Even though it was early November, the dress code meant that I was more appropriately dressed for a warm summer's evening. An off-the-shoulder satin number in muted green with perfectly matched strappy sandals that I could barely walk in, even before I'd had a drink. Teamed with a green and bronze shimmering wrap, my hair newly highlighted and styled in a half-up messy bun, I felt I looked a million dollars. Tim whistled when he saw me and said he'd consider dating me himself if I wasn't such a weirdo.

I had it on good authority that the tickets for this event cost the equivalent of a month's salary for me, so fortunately Tim had provided my ticket free of charge. The venue, Harrington Hotel, was as plush as anywhere I had ever been. Deep pile carpets that felt like marshmallows under my feet, dramatically high ceilings, subdued lighting and eclectically furnished, I felt like I was an extra in an episode of *Downton Abbey*. The waiters and waitresses glided effortlessly through the throng of people like they were ice skating, offering champagne and canapés. After an hour of un-scintillating conversation with some of the towns elite and also boring attendees, we were summoned into dinner in the main dining hall, which also looked like something I'd only ever seen in a film.

There were around forty circular tables, each seating eight guests, with a little place name for everyone. Hence, I ended up with Tim on one side and the gorgeous Will on the other. It seemed Tim and Will vaguely knew one another from some business thing they had both attended, which made the situation a little easier. Will's date, the stunning, stick-thin Felicity, was as charming as she was beautiful, which made it difficult to dislike her, although I did experience a pang of something distasteful, perhaps envy, based on her being a) stunning, b) at least two dress sizes smaller than me and c) Will's date for the evening.

At some point, after copious amounts of champagne, I tottered to the powder room, only to come across Felicity, on her phone, whispering through gritted teeth. As she hadn't noticed me, I went about my business and discreetly washed my hands as she said, "To hell with you, Adrian, I have no intention of putting up with any more of your narcissistic behaviour, I will arrange for Will to collect the rest of my things over the weekend. Goodbye." She ended the call, and our eyes met in the mirror as a tear ran down her immaculately made-up cheek.

What does one say at this point? "Are you okay? Sorry,

obviously not, and it's none of my business, is there anything I can do?" was all I could come up with at short notice.

"Bless you, sweetie, I'll be fine now I'm shot of that bloody man. Could you let my brother know I'll be a minute, and ask him to get me a large brandy please?"

I'm not proud of my inner reaction. I was delighted she was not Will's girlfriend, but the timing was a little off. Fortunately, my face was behaving itself for once, and I think I maintained a look of sympathy and concern. I returned to the table and passed on the message to Will, who thanked me and muttered, "Bloody Adrian, I'll bet," under his breath. Not me, I'm not a gossip – well, maybe a little bit – but I had relayed the exact message from Felicity. So, either Will is psychic, or he knew the history. Felicity returned with a fresh coat of lipstick and mascara, and the rest of the evening got under way. After a five-course meal fit for a king, Felicity insisted that Will swap places with me so we could get to know each other better, and the men could talk 'the boring stuff that men talk about', which made me smile – Tim is far from boring.

I missed the clue right there.

The auction got underway, and I was gobsmacked and horrified simultaneously. Who has two thousand eight hundred pounds to fritter away on a luxury weekend in the Lake District? Not even in a nice hotel, it's a lakeside cabin, so you'd have to take your own supplies.

An England football shirt, signed by some of the players I've never even heard of fetched over seven thousand pounds. A bottle of wine, donated and signed by some retired cricketer £1,660. How the other half live, eh? If I had that sort of money, I'd be wearing Christian Louboutin shoes, a different pair for every day of the week. Obviously, I'd bid on something at the auction, but it would be something that I know someone else would outbid me on. I've done my bit by buying a ticket in the first place. Okay, I hear you, Tim paid for that!

It was a fun evening, and I knew I'd made a new friend with Felicity, who had invited me over for Sunday lunch at her parents' the following weekend. What I didn't realise was that I was also being set up, as was Will, as Felicity had decided I was perfect girlfriend material for him, and thought she'd get the parents on side early doors. As it happened, Audrey and Cecil agreed with their daughter, and before I knew what had hit me, Will and I had our first date, the first of many, as it turned out.

Will is the perfect gentleman: attentive, kind, thoughtful and easy on the eye. Our first date was to the theatre to see a show I'd mentioned to Felicity I really wanted to see, so ten points right there, Will. It was magical, and afterwards we went for a late supper at Andre's; you know the place, costs an arm and two legs for a glass of wine. Goodness knows what the lobster and gruyere quiche cost. Will wouldn't hear of me paying for anything, thankfully. It was one of those 'too much month left at the end of the money' times for me.

Although our dates were regular, they were usually on a weekend, as Will commuted to London most days. There

was some confusion when he told me he was a barrister –
there goes my free coffee! I'm kidding, obviously. It took
a while before I realised that most of our dates revolved
around places I would like to go. Will was very obliging and
eager to please, but I didn't really find out much about him
or what he would like to do. Although I enjoyed going out
with Will, I did feel somewhat guilty that the world seemed
to revolve around me and my needs and wants. I lost count
of the number of times I asked Will what he would like
to do or where he would like to go. We often went out to
dinner with various friends or business colleagues of Will's,
but I was beginning to realise that he didn't seem to have
many real friends or hobbies or interests. When I asked
him what he did with his evenings in London, he said he
mostly spent his evenings working on the following day's
cases. I began to feel the relationship was very one sided.
Will was happy to cater for my needs but didn't seem to
need anything from me other than companionship. One
particular evening, we went to a party for my friend's
birthday, and I had a few to drink and ended up laughing
my head off at something silly when I suddenly caught
Will's eye. He was not laughing, not even smiling and
suddenly the penny dropped. I don't think Will had ever
made me laugh or I him. I realised in that moment how
important humour was to me and that there was none in
our relationship.

I knew there and then there was no future for us. I felt
very sad as I looked back over the last few months. One of
my friends had remarked that I had become less fun than

I used to be, and I realised it was because I had become accustomed to adapting to Will's personality. My life has always been somewhat crazy, and a lot of fun and I realised there was none of that in my relationship with Will. Suddenly Felicity's comment at the charity auction about boring men talking about boring men things made perfect sense, Will, as lovely as he is, was boring and she knew it. I found it hard to end the relationship with Will because he had done nothing wrong, always charming, always laid back, but the truth is, he just was not much fun to be with. I think Felicity was more upset than either me or Will, but we have remained friends, and I think she realises it was not meant to be. Maybe I am a little immature, feeling I need to be entertained by a prospective partner but, quite honestly, if there's no laughter and fun in the relationship then I'm out.

Will is a pair of plain black pumps, you know the ones like ballet slippers. They quietly go with whatever you're wearing but they never make a statement. There was a pair in my wardrobe once, I can't imagine why. My shoes, as you've probably worked out, are usually the star of the show, something poor old Will was never going to be.

Xavier

You will have seen Xavier, I'm sure, maybe not in real life, but on TV, posters in bus stops, advertising boards everywhere, particularly around Christmas and New Year. He's the guy with the beautiful blond curls, matted with blood, lying unconscious in the street next to an overturned car with the wheels still spinning. He's been the 'Don't Drive Drunk' poster guy for the last few years. People think his day job is just as glamorous as his modelling, but he's a paramedic, which is not as glamorous as you'd imagine. You may be surprised to discover that I see Xavier as my jade green kitten heel mules. They are gorgeous to look at and amazingly comfortable, like him. I mean, I wouldn't want to walk three miles in them or wear them all day and evening, but I love them. Like Xavier, they are unusual but cute.

Xavier is one of those amazing people, beautiful inside and out, although he'll hate me for saying so. He is kind to everyone, even the patients he gets called to having an altercation in the street after a few too many beers that proceed to throw up over his boots. He has tolerance for even the most irritating people; he has the view that everyone can be an idiot sometimes and never takes things personally. His training as a paramedic and his natural charm makes him very easy to get along with.

He loves kids, animals and would never even kill a spider, he'd just carry it outside and put it in a safe place. Don't be under the misapprehension that he's a pushover, though. Behind the relaxed attitude and compassion is a man with strong values and opinions that he's not afraid to voice. The twinkling blue eyes can turn steely grey in a heartbeat, piercing like diamonds if someone has overstepped the mark. He's not aggressive or confrontational, just politely very firm, making his point without ever raising his voice.

I witnessed him at his finest when a group of teenagers were outside the coffee shop, being loud and taking the mick out of an elderly lady trying to get in with her walker. After ensuring the lady got safely into the shop, he took the offenders to one side and gave them a real talking to. While I didn't hear most of what he said, I could see he meant business and, within minutes, the lads had gone inside, apologised to the lady, paid for her coffee and cake and offered to help her home with her shopping.

Xavier lives with his nan, so it's no surprise that he's protective of the elderly, I suppose. His parents are alive and well, but when his grandfather died a few years ago, he decided he would live with his nan to ensure she didn't end up in a care home, her worst fear. When he is at work on day shifts, his mother pops round and has lunch with his nan as, due to mobility issues after a stroke, she is unable to get out on her own. When he is on nights, he tucks her up in bed watching *Midsomer Murders* or whatever her latest favourite is and makes sure she's wearing her pendant alarm. He makes out his nan is doing him a huge favour by allowing him to live there; he is saving for a deposit for a house, so the fact that his nan refuses any money apart from paying the grocery bill is a godsend. He also has three sisters still living with their parents, so he calls his nan's house his sanctuary. All of the sisters are lovely, too, going to stay at Nan's when Xavier goes away on holiday.

Apart from his modelling and his paramedic job, he also volunteers at the local animal shelter whenever he can, taking the bigger dogs out that are harder to manage. He even manages to turn that around as if they are doing him a favour. He says he'd never get any decent exercise if it wasn't for the dogs.

So, if Xavier sounds too good to be true, remember that you'll never be a priority, he has a lot of commitments. But who wouldn't love a man who looks after his nan?

Yannis

Okay, I'm cheating a little here. I have never dated Yannis, that would be too weird, as he is a relative in a strange way. Not an actual blood relation but still family. I may have mentioned my somewhat dysfunctional family before, so here's the lowdown on Yanni, as we call him. My aunt, whom I mentioned previously – the one who started my shoe obsession – was, at some point, married to one of her younger men, almost thirty years her junior, who had a son called Yannis from a previous marriage. So, he's kind of a not really cousin, if that makes sense. But family, none the less.

His mother is Greek Cypriot. You can imagine how good looking he is, and of course has fabulous teeth, with a smile that lights up his whole face.

He will not be too impressed I'm telling you this, but his nickname in the family is Twinkle, primarily due to his enormous twinkly brown eyes. He always looks like he's about to burst out laughing (which has been a bit awkward at family funerals when people who haven't met him before are not quite sure why he looks that way). I don't recall him ever laughing at a funeral, to be fair, but it is always there, just under the surface. When he does laugh, it's so infectious that even if you didn't know what the joke was you would find yourself laughing too. It also makes it virtually impossible to be cross with Yanni; he just raises his eyebrow and tilts his head, looking so cute you can't possibly maintain a straight face.

His full nickname is Twinkle-toes, due to his career as a dancer. This may be a disadvantage for any potential girlfriends, as he is completely dedicated to his career, leaving little time or energy for anything else. He is in incredible shape, with a physique I'll leave to your imagination. This has caused a problem with a couple of women he dated previously who were obsessed with their weight, and no matter how hard they tried, were heavier than Yanni. He trains religiously every day for hours, and when he is in a show, can be away for weeks at a time. Don't let his slight frame fool you, Yanni is as strong as an ox. He can still lift me up, and I'm a tad heavier than him. I use the term 'tad' loosely.

Yanni is the silver strappy shoes you would wear if you were competing on *Strictly Come Dancing*: very glittery and covered in diamantés but with a sensible heel height so you don't break an ankle. He seems to sprinkle magic fairy dust wherever he goes; there is something almost childlike in him that makes the people around him feel happy just by being in his presence.

Yanni has a wicked sense of humour, usually at the expense of others. When we were kids, playing in the back garden, he persuaded me to be the princess captured by the bad knight and tied me to a tree so he could play the handsome prince/hero and rescue me. He then went inside for lunch, leaving me tied up for what seemed like hours. Probably only ten minutes later, my mum came running outside to untie me, by which time I was crying my eyes out. Yanni was punished by having to let me play with his action man figure (his prized possession) for a whole weekend. Of course, I hid it in the airing cupboard and couldn't remember where I'd put it. Somehow, we've remained close, even though he dyed my Sindy doll blue with ink and shaved her hair off to repay me.

I think the fact he is a dancer, spending a lot of time with women has made him empathetic and patient; he's my go-to if I have a problem. He can listen for hours, has never called me a drama queen (which I clearly am), and usually comes up with a plan to help me deal with whatever the crisis of the day happens to be. Also, his Christmas gifts are always special. He could remember a conversation we'd had last February about some earrings I'd seen and there they were at Christmas, wrapped up in a beautiful silk kimono he'd found on his travels. He'll never forget your birthday, and even from the other side of the world, he will have left a card and a gift with someone for you, which is always something special that he's clearly thought about. He is the kind of man I would love for a brother; family is everything to him and it shows.

If you can cope with the fact that he will always have a better figure than you, and be a better dancer, maybe Yanni is the man for you.

Zac

You may find Zac a little hard work. He is what my mother would have called 'pernickety'. I think he just likes things done a certain way: his way. You know the type; when you've painstakingly loaded the dishwasher, he will take most of it out and reload it the way he thinks it should be done. If you throw your jacket over the back of the chair, he'll automatically hang it for you 'where it belongs' on a peg in the hall. Don't get me wrong, he doesn't moan, just follows you around tidying up without a word. If you are a little disorganised and wish you weren't, Zac may be for you.

There are advantages to living with Zac. If you use the bathroom, there is not a shred of evidence that anyone has used it since the cleaner last visited. He's only the second man I know that cleans the loo every time he uses the bathroom, and washes his hands, and leaves the towel on the rail exactly as it was. I have never seen so much as a speck of toothpaste in the sink, or an empty loo roll in his house. Makes me wonder why he even has a cleaner, to be honest, I bet he runs around checking everything is exactly as it should be before she arrives.

Immediately after dinner, the dishwasher is loaded (his

way, like I said), the pots are washed, dried and put away and the stove is wiped down (and dried with a microfibre cloth to prevent smears!).

When he makes the bed, I swear he uses a tape measure to make certain the throw is level both sides, and the pillows are the correct angle. I once put one of the bed cushions back upside down for my own amusement. He, however, was not amused. Apparently, I have childish tendencies! Tell me something I don't know!

So, onto the good points. The man can cook, and does he cook? He makes the most amazing risotto I've ever eaten, fantastic curries, tapas, Chinese, and a roast dinner to knock your socks off. You will be wearing socks, obviously, as your shoes must be left at the front door, paired tidily. He's intelligent, well-read and can discuss current affairs in great depth for what seems like hours if that's your thing. Not opinionated, exactly, well okay, he's a little opinionated. In truth, he's a lot opinionated, in my opinion. Not that I'm opinionated at all, of course.

He is very thoughtful. Expect him to always remember special occasions like birthdays and anniversaries without prompting. He managed to get tickets to the grand prix for my birthday, something *he* has always wanted, of course. Then tickets for a Metallica concert… the fact I'm a massive P!NK fan obviously went unnoticed. Like I said, thoughtful, but not necessarily about you.

Zac is not interested in football, rugby, tennis or cricket. He is passionate about motor sport as he thinks there is a level of skill involved in that. Apparently, any idiot can hit or kick a ball about, but it takes expertise to drive a car at speed. He's clearly never seen me on the M4.

Zac is my kitten heel sling-back powder-blue pointed toe shoes, bought on a whim because they looked amazing and I love the colour. They were very expensive and, while I still open the wardrobe and admire them, I know I'll never wear them again; they pinch, they rub, and they make your feet feel like they are on fire after twenty minutes. Like Zac, they seemed like a good idea at the time.

Zac gets the sack

I'm not sure exactly how Zac and I got together. We'd been friends for a long time, and I think we just drifted into being together. I would sometimes stop by on the way home from work to have a chat and a glass of something chilled and sparkling. We took it in turns to have a moan, me usually about work and Zac about Corinna, his ex-girlfriend who had recently moved out but seemed unable to make a complete break. Once or twice, Corinna and I were there at the same time – she also had a habit of just popping in to see how Zac was doing. It was never an issue; she and I had always got on well and had quite a lot in common. I may have had ulterior motives, occasionally, for just stopping by at Zac's. If I hadn't got much in the fridge, or couldn't be bothered to cook, I knew Zac would say, "Hey, I'm just throwing a seafood linguine together, there's plenty. Why not stay and have something with me?

I know you'll go home and eat toast otherwise, and you're looking a bit thin lately, you need something decent to eat." How can you not fall in love with a man who tells you you're thin?

So, I'd perch on a stool in the kitchen while Zac cooked for us, sipping my Chablis and chatting. He'd never let me help clear up afterwards, either. He had a system, he said, and preferred to do it after I'd left, so a win-win for me. Then one evening, I didn't leave. We had drunk way too much for a work night, and it was midnight, so Zac offered me the spare room, which I gratefully accepted. The en-suite to the spare room had a new toothbrush, toothpaste and make-up wipes all laid out, and a phone charger beside the bed. I was impressed. In the morning, I left before Zac was awake, to get a shower and clean clothes at home before work, but sent him a text at lunchtime, thanking him for his hospitality. He replied quickly, "My pleasure, Hannah, I really enjoy your company, so let's do it again soon. X"

It became a regular thing, usually when I had quite a lot of month left at the end of the money, and a sparsely populated fridge, but I always made sure I took wine and chocolate. We'd curl up on the sofa, chatting or watching a movie, totally relaxed in each other's company. Then, one night, he just leant over and kissed the end of my nose and told me I was a strange mixture of cute and beautiful, and someone he'd like to wake up with every day. Within a month, we had set a date for our wedding, in three months' time, I'd rented out my place and moved in with

Zac. The three months flew by, and we married in a quiet ceremony with family and a few close friends. We had a ten-day honeymoon in Santorini, which was everything I dreamt it would be, and then back to reality with a bang. I had known from the pre-wedding months that Zac was, shall we say, houseproud? But living together as a married couple was not how I had envisaged. Zac seemed to follow me around, hanging up my jacket when I'd thrown it on the kitchen stool, taking my magazine from the coffee table and putting it in the rack, even putting the milk back in the fridge before I'd decided if my coffee was milky enough. He didn't moan, or nag, but I was beginning to feel like a child, which turned into me behaving like one, of course. I would leave the light on upstairs, or my keys on the kitchen worktop and see how long it took for him to put things right. It sounds trivial and childish, which it is, I suppose, but I found I was living in a heightened state of anxiety. I'm not particularly untidy, but nor am I someone who must have everything exactly where it lives at all times. Things came to a head when my friend Sophie had been round for dinner one evening. Zac had cooked us one of his legendary risottos, but before we'd swallowed the last mouthful, he was taking our plates to the kitchen to rinse and put in the dishwasher. Sophie had laughed, "No chance of a second helping, then?" But I was embarrassed. And a bit angry. I felt it was bad manners, and he'd made me feel that he couldn't wait for her to go. We discussed it after Sophie had left like reasonable adults, but Zac seemed unable to grasp what I was saying. He just kept repeating that he just likes things cleared away and tidy.

We carried on with our lives, but I was struggling to relax in what was supposed to be my home, and Zac was relentless in his pursuit of the perfect home. On a Sunday, I couldn't have a lie-in because if I went and made a coffee to take back to bed and read, by the time I got back upstairs, the bed was made and the curtains open. We ended up going for counselling a few times, which didn't help. It was suggested we both try 'acceptance' as our mantra and maybe have a separate space that the other one must respect and not make untidy/keep tidying. That didn't work either.

A very sad moment was when the subject of us having a cat or dog was raised (by me, obviously) and Zac's expression was like he'd been seen walking around Tesco naked; he was horrified. It was clear that having children, which really should have been discussed before we got married, was not an option for Zac. I did bring it up, of course, just to be certain, but I was right. Zac said that he'd never even thought about having children, it wasn't something he was even prepared to consider. The mess, the noise, the inconvenience and total disruption having a child would bring were, in his words, not happening in his life. And that was the moment our marriage ended.

Finding the Right Fit

A New Beginning

After two disastrous marriages, I was ready to admit defeat. Marriage and men were off my radar and that was the way it would stay. We are not going where you might be thinking, no thanks, I can honestly say, I have never been attracted to my own sex. So, here I am, a thirty-something single woman, solvent, GSOH, OHAC, OHAT. For those not familiar with this, it stands for good sense of humour, own house and car, and own hair and teeth. In truth, this is borderline on the honesty scale. My sense of humour, I have been told, is a little 'out there', whatever that means. I do find strange things amusing, according to my friends, and am often laughing hysterically at something with other people looking on, completely bemused, which, of course, makes me laugh even more that no one else gets it. Own house, well mostly, but I do have a mortgage the size of Birmingham. Own car, almost. Six months left on the finance plan. Own hair? Well, technically, yes, it is growing out of my own head, but the colour is definitely not my own and I sometimes have some help with extra bits put in. And own teeth? Well, I don't have veneers or anything, or a full set of fake granny gnashers, but I have one implant, courtesy of Poppy McKendall and a fast-moving hockey ball some years ago. She was sent off.

And here I am, rocking singledom like I was born for it. I can buy new shoes whenever I like (another slight exaggeration, it's whenever the credit card says I can), I can watch soppy films eating cheese and jam sandwiches in my PJs on a Sunday afternoon, and I never have to sigh finding the toilet seat up. Of course, at my age, most of my single friends are no longer single – there seem to be husbands and babies popping up all over the place – so my social life is somewhat curtailed by that. I'm certainly not sad and lonely, I enjoy my own company and still have some friends who are either single too, or desperate to escape their husband and children for a few hours. And strangely, some people seem quite envious of my single status. Having retrieved my favourite cushions and other cheap and tacky possessions from my ex-husband, my home is, once again, my sanctuary, and I feel more at peace than I have done for some time.

Until 11.20pm on Sunday 14th May. Let me set the scene for you. I'd had an early bath around six o'clock, left my hair to dry in rats' tails, put on my pyjamas and painted my toenails a rather sickly shade of pink. In fairness, the shade is called cotton candy, so I don't know why I thought it might look nice. I was wrong, and too lazy to redo them, so there I was. I had also had my Chinese takeaway delivered, but was too lazy to get a plate, so had eaten it out of the carton with a fork and left that on the coffee table. A half-drunk bottle of Malbec and empty glass were on the floor next to the sofa, with a dozen Celebrations chocolate wrappers to keep them company. I'm not often prone to being a slob, but everyone needs a night off from being perfect, me included. Anyway, it was a Sunday night, which is sacred, no one visits me on a Sunday evening, everyone knows the rules.

I was watching an old episode of *Midsomer Murders*, my guilty secret pleasure that I've never admitted to anyone, and thinking I should call it a night, when I heard a faint tap-tap-tap on the glass in the front door. I think my heart stopped beating for a few seconds. I crept into the hall, wondering if I had anything useful nearby that could be used as a weapon. Apart from a small Minnie Mouse umbrella (Secret Santa gift from work, thanks, guys) there was nothing.

"Go away or I'll set the dog on you and call the police!" I said loudly to my side of the front door, in the most assertive tone I could muster, which in truth sounded more like Minnie Mouse. The response was the last thing I expected. Whoever was outside was laughing.

"Hannah, I'm sure you know that you don't actually have a dog, and I'm sorry to burst your bubble, but I am the police. It's Oliver. I'm sorry to disturb you but I saw the light on, so assumed you were still up. I have a bit of a problem, and I didn't know what to do."

"What? Oliver? What's happened? Are you okay? What can I do to help?" I was a gibbering idiot.

"You could let me in for a start!" He was laughing again. I opened the door and stood back to let him in.

At this point, I noticed he was soaking wet. "I didn't notice it was raining; you're soaked to the skin, Oliver! Let me get some towels, wait there a second." I raced upstairs to the airing cupboard, grabbing my dressing gown from the bedroom to make myself feel a little less exposed.

By the time I came back, Oliver was wearing just his boxer shorts, with his clothing all piled up on the doormat. To cover my embarrassment, and possibly his, he started cracking jokes. "Well, I could've at least taken you out for dinner first, but I expect you've already eaten." Still in the hallway, Oliver was drying himself and had started to shiver. I led him into the lounge and turned on the gas fire. I took off my dressing gown and gave it to him to wear, while I went to make some coffee.

When I came back with the coffee, Oliver was still shivering violently and looked ashen, the comedian mask slipping. "Just relax and drink your coffee, I'm going to put your clothes in the tumble drier and get you a brandy, I'll be right back."

Although curiosity was killing me, I realised Oliver may be in shock and, although I was worried, thought I'd give him time to regain his composure before interrogating him. I ran upstairs and threw some clothes on, then sorted his clothes for the dryer, feeling like a thief checking the pockets of his jeans, before pouring us both a large brandy.

I put the brandies on the coffee table and sat quietly alongside Oliver on the sofa. He let out a huge sigh and I squeezed his hand. "I'm so sorry to scare you at this time of night, Hannah, I'm not really thinking straight. I've had a couple of drinks. I left the pub intending to go straight home but there was a young lad and his girlfriend having a bit of an argument. It was all getting out of hand, so I discreetly followed them to make sure she was safe. They were on the towpath, and I stayed behind them until he started pushing her. Of course, I intervened, which resulted in her running off, thankfully, before he punched me in the jaw. I'm ashamed to say I overbalanced and fell backwards into the canal. I feel a right idiot. I had my keys and my phone in my hand, so they're somewhere in the murky depths of the canal, never to be seen again. Now I understand why you girls have handbags. I can't get into my house, and I can't phone anyone to ask to stay on their couch."

It was then I saw the swelling on Oliver's jaw and realised it must be painful. I fetched some water and painkillers and made the decision that would change my life.

"For tonight, you can stay here, obviously. And we can worry about tomorrow when it comes. Now, you look like you probably could do with something to eat. I'm no Mary Berry but could throw some baked beans at a couple of slices of toast if that would be okay?" Decision made, we both went into the kitchen and put together beans on toast, and more coffee, with Oliver perched on a bar stool, looking slightly weird in my pink fluffy dressing gown. By the time Oliver had eaten, and we'd tidied the lounge and loaded the dishwasher, it was two o'clock in the morning. I found a new toothbrush, more clean towels and showed

Oliver the spare bedroom and bathroom, reassuring him it was fine to have a shower before going to bed. I did draw the line at offering him any of my underwear, let's not make this any weirder than it is.

The following morning was weird, but in a good way. When I came downstairs, my hair looking like I'd been electrocuted, Oliver was in the kitchen, fully dressed, making coffee for us both. We worked together; I sliced bread while Oliver found the butter and marmalade and we sat together at the breakfast bar, like we had done this a thousand times. We chatted about what Oliver would do next. He'd correctly assumed I was working from home, and had arranged for Andy, his friend, to come and collect him and get things sorted. The house felt strangely quiet after he had gone, and I struggled to knuckle down to work. In the drama of the previous evening, I'd forgotten just how attractive Oliver (my favourite shoes, my sage-green suede mules) was. What I had noticed was the comfortability of being with him. I'm not sure that comfortability is even a real word, but you get my meaning. He'd been in my home for less than twelve hours, but I felt like I was missing him. Most peculiar.

It was four days before I heard from Oliver, if you don't count the thank you card through the letterbox on Tuesday. He knocked on the door early Thursday evening with a beautifully wrapped parcel in his hands, and a bottle of wine.

"I expect you have plans for this evening, so I won't hold you up, I just wanted to thank you for all you did for me on Sunday, you really saved my skin. I brought you a little something as a thank you," he said.

"On the contrary, I was just thinking about what culinary disaster I could throw together tonight! Please come in and at least have a drink, I'm dying to hear the next instalment of your crazy life." I do tend to burble when I'm nervous, and for some reason was feeling strangely shy, a new experience for me.

Oliver followed me down the hall into the kitchen, where I held up a bottle of Sauvignon Blanc in one hand, and a beer in the other, wearing my 'question mark' expression. Thankfully, Oliver opted for the wine, as I was secretly hoping he would, as that meant he would be more likely to stay longer. I know, I'm a bit sad, and devious. As I'd hoped, one glass turned into three and Oliver suggested either a takeaway or that he could rustle up something after inspecting the contents of the fridge. Plan B was a joint decision, and I pulled up a stool to watch the proceedings with interest. I was unaware I was nervously picking at the wrapping on my parcel until he said, "You can open it if you like," and he laughed. On discovering the contents, I laughed too. "I seem to remember you're a Minnie Mouse fan – the umbrella in the hall, and those pyjamas from many years ago. Do you remember? The night you threw your chicken chow mein at me outside the pub. And I called round later to check you were okay? You had Minnie Mouse pyjamas on, and Teletubby slippers."

"Good grief! How embarrassing was that?" I replied. "I know you're a police officer, but your powers of observation from way back then are ridiculous. You could have saved my blushes and pretended you'd forgotten all about it. However, the Minnie Mouse dressing gown is gorgeous, so thank you, and I forgive you for remembering. And thanks for not arresting me for crimes against fashion." We were both still laughing when the smoke alarm went off.

"How do you like your salmon, burnt or black? I call this dish 'double-charred delight'; it's my signature dish, you know," he joked. It was delicious when we'd scraped off the burnt bits. We ate the salmon with some ratatouille, and drank the rest of the wine, chatting all the while about our work, our friends and people we both knew. Before I knew what was going on, it was well after midnight.

"Well, that's twice I've eaten here, so if you're up for it, I'd like to take you out for a proper dinner somewhere nice, as a real thank you whenever you're free. Not that beans on toast or burnt salmon aren't proper dinners, obviously, I'm sorry that sounded awful. I would really like to take you out, not just to say thank you, but because I like you and really enjoy spending time with you." He actually blushed, bless him.

"I'd really like that too, Oliver, so thank you. There's a new tapas restaurant on the quay, have you been there? Maybe, if you like tapas, we could try that?" Look at me, cool, calm and collected. I could feel an Oscar coming my way. We agreed on the following Monday for our tapas evening as Oliver was working all weekend and he gave me a peck on the cheek as he left. I danced round the kitchen singing Queen's 'Don't Stop Me Now' at the top of my voice when the face appeared at the kitchen window. Oliver had left his keys on the kitchen island. Absolutely mortified, I opened the back door and handed him the keys.

"Night, Freddie, looking forward to Monday," he said with a grin, and disappeared into the darkness.

I floated through the next few days in a cloud, then remembered I was recently divorced, and had made a pact with myself to stay away from men for the foreseeable future. Should I cancel our date? Was it even a date or just old friends having dinner together? Was I heading for another romantic disaster and a broken heart? Or was I about to pass up a date with Oliver because I was scared of what might (or worse, might not) happen? By the time Monday came around, my brain felt like it had been in the washing machine on fast spin. I decided to go for it, relax and just enjoy his company. Easier said than done, obviously. I took the afternoon off work and popped into town, treated myself to a new pair of shoes, some sunglasses, as I was finding it too bright, a mascara, and some gorgeous green underwear. Not that anyone was going to see the underwear, of course, but I always think pretty underwear makes you feel special, and who knows when I'll be hit by a bus and have to be undressed in the back of an ambulance?

I had a soak in the bath, while deciding what to wear. The new underwear, new shoes, and my favourite jeans and a white top. Not the sunglasses, obviously; although I was struggling with bright lights, I didn't want to look like a diva. My hair, unfortunately, has a mind of its own and decided to go into 'very badly behaved mode', along the lines of Tina Turner in a force ten gale. Knowing it was hopeless trying to do anything when it's in that mood, I scraped most of it into a clip and put on some nice earrings to try to deflect attention from the hair. A couple of coats of mascara, a neutral lip gloss, new shoes, keys, phone, bag and I was good to go.

Oliver arrived by taxi bang on time, and we set off. He was very complimentary. "Looking good, Freddie, love the shoes. And you've done something different with your hair, it suits you." If anyone else had said that I'd have thought they were taking the mickey but that's not Oliver, he missed the sarcasm gene completely.

As first dates go, it turned out to be memorable. We discovered we both liked the same foods, we liked Rioja, and we had a similar sense of humour. We ended up like giggling schoolkids when the woman at the next table was trying out her Spanish on the waiter who, unfortunately, was from Walsall and couldn't understand a word she was saying. After we had ordered coffee and churros, my right eye started to feel itchy, and I was trying not to rub it when Oliver asked if I was all right. Apparently, my eye had started to swell, and I looked like I'd been crying. I excused myself and went to check in the ladies. Well, Oliver was certainly the master of understatement; I looked like something out of a horror movie. I ran some cold water and soaked a tissue to try and reduce the swelling, but to no avail.

By the time I returned to the table, I could hardly see. The bill had been paid, a taxi was waiting for us outside and Oliver instructed the driver to take us to A&E. My vision had been a bit blurry all day, and I had been struggling with the lighting in the restaurant but had tried to ignore it. I told Oliver it was probably a reaction to my new mascara, and I should just go home and take it off, but he was insistent and would not take no for an answer, so we went to hospital. Luck was certainly on my side that night, as A&E was unusually quiet, and I was triaged within minutes. Oliver refused to leave me there, so waited patiently while I was seen in a cubicle by a lovely nurse called Paul. After a hundred questions and a thorough examination, Paul decided to call the duty eye doctor as he told me eye casualty was closed till the morning and this couldn't wait. I started to panic, but Paul was kind and reassuring. He suggested having my husband come in and wait with me, and I was so freaked out I didn't correct him, I just nodded my agreement. When the eye doctor came in, he asked all the questions again: Did I wear contact lenses? Had I suffered any trauma to my eye recently? He then informed me I had a corneal ulcer, which is a medical emergency and can result in permanent blindness in the eye if not diagnosed and treated promptly. I was told to come back to eye casualty at eight o'clock in the morning and was discharged with eye drops to be administered every hour for twenty-four hours.

Oliver was a superhero. He organised a taxi back to my house, and point-blank refused to leave me. He made us a cup of tea and informed me that not only was he staying the night, but he had also set the alarm on his phone and would administer the eye drops for me as directed by the doctor. So, while he did see my lovely new underwear, it was only as I quickly got undressed. And though we did sleep together, there was certainly no romance, as he slept on top of the bed, fully clothed, getting up every single hour and gently waking me to put the drops in. I remember thinking if I hadn't committed to singledom forever this man would be a keeper.

Oliver woke me at six for my eyedrops, told me he had run me a bath as he was worried about water getting in my eye if I showered, and raced home to get his car to take me back to the hospital. The doctor in eye casualty was very confident the eye would make a full recovery, provided I continued the treatment recommended and had regular checks. And I was to wear sunglasses whatever the weather for a few days, too. "Absolutely no eye make-up for the time being. And nothing but warm water to clean your eye. Your husband has my permission to make sure you do as you're told, young lady. If he hadn't insisted on bringing you in, it may have been a different story. You are very lucky. See the receptionist on the way out and she'll book you in for a follow-up appointment." I thanked him, blushing furiously, and smiled.

"Well, Mrs, let's find somewhere for a nice breakfast." Oliver grinned at me. I blushed again. "I'll be glad to get out of here; I'm not a fan of hospitals. Spend too much time here with burglars who have fallen off ladders and drunken idiots who've got into a punch-up," he said. "Talking of work, I'll need to go home after breakfast to get some sleep before my run of night shifts. Will you be okay?"

I slipped my arm through his as we walked back to the car. "Of course. And thank you for all you've done. You're a star and I really appreciate it. Like the doctor said, it could have turned out very differently if you weren't so bossy." He laughed, leant down and kissed the end of my nose.

After an excessively large breakfast and three cups of coffee, Oliver dropped me home, promising he'd call when he could. I suddenly felt strangely lonely, not a feeling I'm used to. I decided it was sensible to take a day or two off work, as my vision was not at its best. As an interior designer, a keen eye is required, and mine was temporarily not keen to do anything. Within an hour, I realised I'd checked my phone at least three times, so I gave myself a stern talking to, put it in the kitchen and took myself back upstairs to bed.

Surprisingly, I slept, and woke up around two o'clock feeling grateful that my hourly eye-drop was over. Although still blurry, uncomfortable and photosensitive, I was relieved that things were heading in the right direction with my eye. I pottered around all afternoon, catching up on laundry and other chores, feeling a bit disorientated but couldn't work out why. Around six o'clock, I heard my phone ringing in the kitchen; it was Oliver.

"Hey, Freddie, how are you getting on? Just thought I'd check in on you, and see if there's anything you need before I head off to work?"

"Thanks, Oliver, I've had some sleep and I'm doing okay. I'm just making something to eat and going to watch a film on TV. How about you? Did you sleep?"

Oliver confirmed he had slept all afternoon and was just getting ready for his night shift and said goodbye, promising he'd call soon. Again, I started to feel a bit flat, and it took me a while to realise why. I was wishing he wasn't working, and that we could have spent the evening together. Not a feeling I was accustomed to, or happy about. I was in my thirties, happily single and planning to stay that way for the foreseeable future. I needed a distraction, so I did what I do best, found my iPad and started browsing. A handbag, a jacket and three pairs of shoes later, I sent myself to bed early as a punishment.

Mum knows Best

Unsurprisingly, I did not sleep well. My eye was irritating, as was my mind. I felt as though I were at a crossroads: should I nip this Oliver situation in the bud before I get in too deep? Or just go with the flow and see what happens? Once bitten, twice shy. Or in my case, twice bitten, obviously. Or behave like a teenager, recklessly letting my emotions run away with me? After tossing and turning for what seemed like hours, I made a decision to get up, have coffee and a shower and go and see my mother. My mother is a remarkable woman, widowed twice but always upbeat and positive, with an energy and zest for life befitting a woman half her age. She has also had probably more than her fair share of boyfriends, for want of a better term, and is a wise woman on affairs of the heart.

"Darling girl! What a lovely surprise, but what's happened to your eye? That looks very uncomfortable. Come on in, there's a pot of coffee on, and I have those little lemon cakes you love. You're not dieting, are you? No? Silly question, you look fabulous and certainly don't need to worry about your weight. I've been trying that new Heather Hughes eating plan, it's done wonders for Abby, you know my friend across the hallway. She's lost ten pounds and swears by it. It's early days but I certainly feel a difference already! And my new hip has healed perfectly; I'll be back dancing before the end of the month." She twirled on the spot to prove her point.

My mother is what some people would call extrovert; she is enthusiastic about almost everything and borderline theatrical. She can talk without pausing for breath for ages, and has opinions on everything under the sun, but she's the best mum ever. Always there if you need her but never interfering or offering her opinion unless asked. Mind you, if you ask her advice or opinion on anything, be prepared to hear the raw truth. Mum is famous for being a straight talker, so if you're a bit sensitive, ask someone else's advice. My sister once asked Mum if she liked her new dress, and the response was brutal: "Well, the style is far too old for you, darling, and the colour makes you look like you have food poisoning. Your shoes are gorgeous, though." That's my mum, telling it like it is. And perceptive, too.

"So, what brings you here this morning, darling? Boyfriend problems?" She poured the coffee and set out the cakes. No point trying to hide anything from her, so I explained my dilemma in full. "And you are here because you want my advice, I'm assuming? Honestly, you are a funny creature, so like your father it makes me smile."

My father, Mum's first husband, died in his thirties, when I was twelve, and my sister was eight. My memories of him are limited, but I know he was a quiet man with a ready smile, and he loved my mother and us girls beyond measure.

"I'm not like Dad, I'm not quiet at all. I'd say I'm more you, a bit of a party animal and loud," I countered.

"On the contrary, my darling, your father knew how to have a good time, but unlike me, he knew when to stay quiet. He never rushed into anything without looking at the situation from every angle, and weighing up the pros and cons. He thought everything through carefully, before committing to making a decision, exactly what you are doing now. When your dad and I first met, I knew within the first hour that he was the man I wanted to marry. Your darling father, of course, took nearly two years to deliberate before he asked me to marry him. He was lucky I didn't run off with Stan Hardiman, who would have married me in a heartbeat, but there we are. And look what happened when Stan did marry – that poor girl, five children in seven years and then he ran off with that floozy from the bakery. I made the right decision, waiting for your dad to make a decision. We were so happy, you know. No one could hold a candle to your father or ever will."

Finally, she paused long enough for me to chip in. "So, what do you think I should do?" I forgot to tell you, my mum thinks in pictures, and often uses food in her analogies.

"Well, here's my take on the situation. You like fish – in fact, it was always your favourite – so you had a piece of haddock, which looked tasty but was full of bones and somewhat overcooked and dry. It put you off fish for a while. Eventually, you started eating fish again, and it was okay, but not very exciting. One day, you had some smoked mackerel, but unbeknown to you, it was previously frozen and over-defrosted in the microwave. As a consequence, you got food poisoning and were quite ill. This put you off fish again, understandably. Now, you've had a long while to get over it, but it has left you a bit anxious about trying fish again, apart from your favourite salmon. And now you are being offered a beautiful piece of halibut; it looks delicious and is perfectly cooked. Do you refuse to eat it, just in case it is not how it looks? Or do you trust that it may be the best piece of fish you have ever eaten?"

"So, my first marriage was to a haddock, and my second husband was gone-off smoked mackerel? Mum, you are a bit weird, but I get what you're saying. But what if I eat the halibut and it's not very nice, after all? Are we really having this conversation?" I was laughing.

"You have other options, of course. You could give up fish completely, and live on cheese sandwiches, lasagne and shepherd's pie. But think what you might be missing. Remember when I tried blue cheese for the first time? I loved it and was devastated I'd never been brave enough to try it until I was in my forties. You have to try new things, or you'll never know if you like them. And if you try it and don't like it, it's not the end of the world. So, the real question is, are you hungry enough to go for the halibut or are you going to play it safe with the sandwich and risk missing out?"

"Two failed marriages isn't a great track record, Mum. I know we're not that far up the road, but I can't risk getting so involved that it will be heartbreaking. And I'm not good at being married. In fact, I feel a complete failure." I burst into tears.

Mum pushed a box of tissues across the counter to me and took a breath. "You, my darling, are not perfect, of course, none of us are. However, it takes two to make a marriage work, but only one to screw it up. Remember that thing your dad used to say: if we're all peeing out the tent, no one gets wet. But only one person needs to pee in the tent and everyone gets wet. Something like that, anyway. It doesn't matter how hard you work at a relationship, if the other person is not working at it, the relationship is doomed. And that's why things didn't work out when you were married. Accept where you went wrong too and learn from it. You will be surprised to hear that my second marriage to Bill was not a bed of roses. Your dad was a tough act to follow, and I didn't realise how much pressure I put on Bill, expecting things to be like being married to your dad. Poor Bill, we would have probably divorced if he hadn't got ill. I cared for him, as you know, but it wasn't how it should have been. I nursed him until he died because he was a good man, and I was his wife, but I didn't love him by then."

I had no idea, having already left home when she married Bill. I assumed they were happy; there was no sign of anything to the contrary. When I pointed this out to her, my mother was uncharacteristically quiet for a few moments.

"Don't misunderstand me, I wasn't unhappy, exactly, and nor was Bill. We just never had the kind of relationship that your father and I had experienced, I always felt there was something missing. Which there was, from both sides, I think. How can I explain it better? Your father was everything I both wanted and needed in my life, he knew me inside and out, and loved me unconditionally, despite my shortcomings. Of course, we disagreed at times, even had blazing rows occasionally, but there was something, like an invisible thread, that kept us together. When he died, I was devastated but had to hold it together for you and your sister and that was the hardest thing I've ever had to do. But you were a piece of him, and I was so grateful to have that to hang on to. You girls were my lifeboat in a stormy ocean for a long time. When I met Bill, who was like an island in that ocean, I believed that marrying him was the right thing to do. It was very selfish of me, because I was lonely and sad, and needed someone to lean on after the years struggling on my own. Bill offered security and he did love me, but he couldn't give me what I really wanted, which was what I'd had with your dad. People can only give you what they have, and Bill didn't have what I needed. I feel horrible saying this, but it may help you in your life. Figure out what is important to you, what you can tolerate in a relationship, like someone who never puts the lid on the toothpaste, and what your non-negotiables are. For me, I need to be with someone who loves and accepts me for who I am and doesn't want me to change. Bill often criticised me for talking too much, laughing too loudly, or wearing clothes that were too bright. I criticised him for many things, too, and it became almost a competition at times, of who had the most faults.

That's one reason I'm on my own now. I'm happy with who I am, warts and all, and although I'm content to date now and then, I prefer to live on my own. More coffee, darling?"

We sat and talked for another hour, and when I left, I felt I knew my mother much better as a real person, not just as my mum. I also realised how very lucky I was to have her and told her so.

I went home and spent the afternoon cleaning the house. I always resort to housework when I have a lot to think about, so having this dilemma was, in many ways, a bonus. I even cleaned the windows, although I drew the line at cleaning the oven; some jobs can wait. I was no further forward when, on Friday evening, I received a text from Oliver asking if I would be free on Saturday evening, as he'd like to cook dinner for me at his place. My heart did a little flip, which I wasn't sure was a good thing, but I replied in the affirmative.

Saturday dawned bright and cold, so I took myself for a bracing walk along the canal path in the morning to try and calm my mind, before meeting my oldest friend Louisa for lunch.

I picked a quiet corner booth at Barney's and perused the menu while waiting for Louisa. She arrived like the whirlwind she is, breathless and laughing. "Hey, lovely! Am I late? Of course I am, I'm always late, sorry. Grant had borrowed my car, and couldn't remember where he put the keys, and I know I didn't drive here, it's less than a mile, but my house keys are on the same keyring and Grant will be at the rugby when I get back, so I'd be locked out!" Louisa often reminds me of my mother with her ability to speak in full paragraphs without pausing for breath. She struggled out of her jacket and slid in opposite me, still laughing.

"What's going on with you? You look different somehow, and you only twiddle your hair when you have something on your mind. Oh my God! Hannah! Are you pregnant?" Unfortunately, Louisa is also quite loud, so while my cheeks turned into tomatoes, I gestured wildly to lower her voice as I noticed other diners looking over at us curiously.

"Firstly, absolutely not. Secondly, if I was, the whole flipping town would know by now if I was, big mouth! Here, read the menu. I'm having the mango and halloumi salad, and a large glass of Sauvignon Blanc, and you're paying as you've embarrassed me so badly!"

Lou looked appropriately shamefaced, although still grinning like a lunatic. The waitress came and took our order, which gave us a temporary respite.

"I'm sorry, Han, but you do look different in some way… is there a new man? It's not a new hairdo, you still look like you've been in a force ten gale like always." We are not friends because Louisa is subtle, obviously, but I love her nonetheless.

"Louisa, we have been friends since we were seven years old, and I love you dearly. That said, you are a terrible gossip, and you're well known for your inability to keep a secret. But, I'll tell you anyway. I'm dating Norman the storeman from the pet shop."

Norman is at least seventy years old, and is known locally as Spiderman, due to his extensive knowledge and vast collection of pet spiders. He has spider tattoos, wears tarantula T-shirts and is more than a little strange, although harmless.

"Not true, I happen to know Norman is gay, although he is definitely your type."

"Hmm, okay, I'm having an affair with your dad?" Fortunately, Louisa and I share a weird sense of humour, she's never offended.

"Nope, my dad hates you, he says your nose is too big and ugly!" By this time, we are snorting with laughter. I'm no longer worried that other customers are staring, we have reverted to type and our conversation gets more and more ridiculous. Our food arrives and I thank my lucky stars that we have a reprieve. We both love our food and, thankfully, Louisa has the decency to allow us to enjoy eating in peace for a while.

"Right then, I get three guesses, and you have to tell the truth," Louisa announces. "You're getting back with irritating Zac? No, that's beyond impossible. Even you aren't that mad. Oooh, is it a woman you're seeing?" We're snorting with laughter again, remembering Teresa Womack declaring undying love for me when very drunk at her eighteenth birthday party. "You've finally snared Oliver in your evil talons? Oh my God, you have! I can't believe it, you've been obsessed with him forever. Tell me everything!"

I'm actually speechless at this point. Partly because Louisa has rumbled me, and partly because, in her excitement, she has knocked over her Sauvignon Blanc and it's dripping into my lap. After a brief interlude, during which time I escape to the loo and try to dry my trousers with the hand dryer (pretty difficult when you're as short as me), we resume our conversation. In truth, it was more a case of Louisa resuming her interrogation than a conversation. I let her fire questions non-stop for at least five minutes before she realised I hadn't said a word.

"Hannah, you haven't answered a single question. Come on, tell me, please?"

After pointing out that she hadn't paused for breath long enough to get a response, I gave her the barest details. "Oliver had a problem, I helped him out and we've been out to dinner. Not a hint of romance, no gory details to spill, just friends having dinner. And that, my nosey, lovely friend, is all you're going to get, because that is all there is."

Louisa slumped back in her seat with a look of disbelief. I signalled for the bill and the waitress came over.

"My friend here is paying today," I said with a smile, and waited until Louisa had paid and the waitress had moved away. "Sorry to rush off but I have an appointment with my therapist. Today we're covering 'how to deal with nosey friends'. Could be an expensive session. See you soon, darling, love you!"

"You too, sweetie, but call me or text if there's anything to report. I mean anything: if Oliver so much as sneezes, I need to hear about it. Bye!"

Due to the fact my trousers were still very damp, and I was embarrassed, I took a taxi home. And yes, I was worried about bumping into you-know-who looking like I had bladder issues. I spent the afternoon having a long hot soak in the bath, trying to relax.

My eye was almost back to normal, so I took a chance with minimal mascara, and tried in vain to tame the hair. After the steam in the bathroom, the curls were now looking like corkscrews growing out of my head at right angles, so I resorted to putting it up again, rather than frighten Oliver to death with my natural look.

I decided to walk to Oliver's, a decision I regretted after a few hundred metres when it started to rain. My hair likes rain about as much as it likes steamy bathrooms. Strappy pink high-heeled suede shoes were also a bad idea. By the time I arrived, I was very wet indeed.

"Well, hello, Freddie! Did you fall in the canal too? But hey, I'm happy you might need to take some clothes off to get dry, puts us on a more level playing field, doesn't it?" Oliver was trying not to laugh at my dishevelled appearance and failing miserably. I started to laugh too.

"I thought I'd walk over without considering checking the weather; very silly, I know."

Oliver ushered me inside, produced two towels and directed me to the bathroom while finding me a T-shirt and a pair of jogging bottoms that were at least five sizes too big and made for someone at least a foot taller than me. My hair was now having a full-on tantrum, so I resigned myself to looking like a freak and made my way to the kitchen, saying a silent thank you that I'd at least had a pedicure.

A large glass of perfectly chilled Chablis was waiting for me on the kitchen counter, along with Oliver who was obviously not on the counter but standing in front of it, wrapping asparagus in Parma ham and sprinkling them with parmesan cheese.

"I remember you saying you like asparagus, so it's something to pick at while dinner is cooking. I'll just put them under the grill for a few minutes. I remember you also like salmon, so I've taken the liberty of assuming you like all fish. I've prepared some halibut in a lemon and herb butter sauce, is that okay?"

For the second time that day, I was speechless. Then I started laughing. Oliver looked puzzled.

"I'm sorry, yes, that sounds delicious Oliver, thank you. It's just something my mother was saying about halibut, it's a bit of a coincidence, that's all. One of those 'you had to be there' moments."

"How is your mother? She had a hip replacement, didn't she? I bet she was up dancing or playing football within a week. She's a remarkable lady, your mother." I liked the fact that Oliver not only remembered my mum, but he had also listened when I'd spoken about her operation, and he thought she was remarkable, which, of course, she is. The conversation flowed easily, the halibut was out of this world and the evening was relaxed and fun. And not once did Oliver mention my crazy hair. Suddenly it was one o'clock in the morning and I realised I needed to get home.

"Well, now, we have a predicament, Freddie. We'll

never get a taxi at this time in the morning, so here are the options. I can walk you home wearing my clothes but in your bare feet, I can walk you home in your wet clothes and wet shoes, or you can stay over, but I'm afraid there is no spare bedroom." He raised his eyebrow as a question.

I did not walk home.

Do I Like Halibut?

I have long suspected my mother is a witch, or at least has some sort of psychic powers, and my suspicions were exacerbated on Sunday afternoon when she sent me a text message.

"Hello, darling, how was the halibut?" with a winking emoji. I was so freaked out I didn't respond for a couple of hours. Instead, I took my frustration out on a pile of ironing that had been loitering for some time. Eventually, she texted again. "Stop sulking, Hannah, I'm your mother. It's my job to check up on you. I don't need the details, of course, but if you left his house at 11.30 this morning with wild woman hair it's a bit of a giveaway that you stayed overnight." And this time, a laughing emoji.

Having your mother checking up on your love life at my age is embarrassing, but I know she's just being a caring mother, and I was keen to find out how and what she knew, so I called her.

"Hi, Mum, thank you for your nosiness, which I will interpret as caring on this occasion. Yes, I stayed at Oliver's because I'd got soaked to the skin on the way there. He lent me some clothes, which I couldn't walk home in with no shoes. We had a lovely evening, and yes, we have arranged to see one another again soon. How do you know I stayed the night? And how the heck did you know we had halibut for dinner?" I heard a giggle in the background.

"And thank you for putting me on speaker, so Gossipy Grace can join in with the assessment of my love life. Hey, Grace, how are you?"

My sister had the grace to sound sheepish (terrible pun, I know). "Sorry, Han, should have announced my presence. I'm good, thanks. Sounds like you are, too. I called round to see Mum and that Abby woman from across the hall was here, telling Mum she'd seen you this morning, leaving a house in Cross Street kissing a man goodbye. And that your hair looked like it hadn't seen a brush for weeks. Oh, the shame of it! How will we ever live this down?" Grace was laughing loudly now, as was Mum.

"As a matter of fact, darling," Mum chipped in, "I had no idea you had halibut for dinner, but don't you think it's an omen after our conversation yesterday? Quite spooky. And if the man in question is who I think it is, I'm delighted. I just hope I don't slip up and call him Hal when you bring him round." Now we were all laughing. After swearing Grace and Mum to secrecy, I said goodbye and went upstairs for a shower, and to give my hair a good talking to.

The following week was tedious; work was difficult, I didn't see Oliver as he was away on a course, I was feeling flat and finding it difficult to apply myself to anything. So, on Thursday afternoon, I decided to repaint the bathroom, more as a distraction than because it needed painting. Normal people buy tester pots and try out different shades before committing to a colour, but not me. Straight in with the most disgusting shade of pink, I believe Americans call it bubble gum. As design is apparently my forte, and how I earn a living, I'd obviously had some sort of loss of direction, or temporary insanity. Maybe there was a full moon, who knows? By now, it was after eight o'clock in the evening, so I'd have to wait until the morning to rectify the damage. I sat on the edge of the bath, paintbrush in hand, feeling rather foolish and a bit annoyed with myself. My phone was vibrating on the sink. Great time for a video call, Oliver!

"Hello, Freddie, how are you doing? Oh my goodness, what have you done to your hair? Loving the pink ends, very *Vogue*! You match the bathroom walls. They're erm… very pink!" I was at the point of bursting into tears or laughing hysterically, but before I could decide which, Oliver sensed I wasn't in my right mind.

"Listen, we've wrapped up early here and I should be back by midnight. I'm off tomorrow and the weekend. Why don't I come round in the morning and help fix it? I'm assuming you hate it. We could go out for breakfast if you're not working, you can choose a different colour, and we'll have it sorted in a few hours. If you'd like that, of course, I don't want to overstep the mark!"

"Thank you, Oliver, I would like that. If you're not exhausted from your course, it would be lovely to see you, and I would really appreciate some help. I've had a bit of a strange week, and this is the final straw, I've lost my mind, I think."

"I'll try and help you find that, too, but I fear that might be gone forever. How's 8.30am sound? Not too early?" We said our goodbyes and I realised I was smiling again.

The next morning, I felt lighter, like the cloud that had been hovering over me all week had lifted. Oliver was on time, smiling behind a huge bouquet of white roses. We went to a small independent café for breakfast and spent a leisurely hour catching up on each other's news over coffee and a delicious breakfast of poached eggs and avocado on sourdough toast.

"You know something, Freddie? This might sound strange, but this just feels right, us relaxed and chatting over breakfast. I feel so comfortable around you, I never have to think about what I should or shouldn't say. I don't want to jinx things, or rush you into anything you're not ready for, but I need you to know that my hope is this relationship continues going from strength to strength. I know you've had some bad experiences in the past, but I don't want to think that would stop us from having a future together. You're special, Freddie, and you are important to me."

Yet again, I found myself speechless for a few moments. I reached across the table and squeezed Oliver's hand. He looked a little embarrassed, sitting with his head down, so I said, "Thank you for that, Oliver, I really enjoy spending time with you, too, and I know I err on the side of caution where relationships are concerned but just give me time. Let's live in the moment and see where life takes us. I admit, I'm a little scared, it's not easy to trust again, but I'm getting there. And this is quite an admission for me: I missed you this week."

Oliver smiled and took my other hand. "That is good enough for me. Come on, then, my little pink-haired pixie, let's buy some paint and get to work."

By five o'clock, the bathroom was restored to its former glory: white. We hadn't eaten since breakfast, so I suggested a takeaway and a glass of wine. Over dinner, Oliver told me it was his twin nephews' birthdays on the Sunday and asked how I would feel about accompanying him to his brother's for the afternoon.

"I'll understand if you're not comfortable with it. My parents will be there, my brother Scott and his wife Michelle and the two boys, Kent and Ricky, who will be four. They are all great people, and I think you'll love them, but no pressure. I have told them about you, but said we are taking things slowly. Have a think about it."

"Okay, I've had a think and yes please, I'd love to come." I immediately wondered whether it was really me speaking but, as there was no one else in the room, I must have said it. I'm a big fan of acting on impulse, that's why I have so many pairs of shoes.

I drew the line at having Oliver put my name on his gifts for the twins, but I did ask his advice on what to buy them myself, and settled on a puzzle each, a dinosaur one for Kent and an astronaut one for Ricky. I also bought flowers for Michelle and a nice bottle of Malbec. Sunday dawned bright and sunny, reflecting my mood and Oliver's optimism for what the day would bring. After at least four outfit changes, and a full-blown argument with my hair, I settled on a white top and my favourite jeans with flats, with my hair tied back and minimal make-up.

"Freddie, you look stunning. And don't look so nervous, I know my family will love you as much as I do." There was an awkward silence, and I focused on locking the front door until the moment passed. Oliver drove us to his brother's house, a beautiful Victorian semi on the outskirts of town, and we arrived to find everyone in the back garden, the twins running around pretending to be flying and the adults sitting on the patio with a glass of wine.

"Hello everyone, I'd like you to meet Hannah. Freddie, my parents Jack and Sylvia, Scott my brother, and my favourite sister-in-law Michelle."

Handshakes were overlooked in favour of hugs, which instantly made me feel relaxed, and Michelle said, "Looks like I'll always be Oliver's favourite sister-in-law seeing as Scott is his only brother!" She laughed and offered me a drink. We sat and chatted for a few minutes. It was obvious Oliver had told them about me from their questions about my work, my mother's recovery after her operation and general chat. Suddenly, the twins realised their uncle had arrived and he was almost knocked out of his chair by their exuberance.

"Uncle Wally! Uncle Wally, I'm four now, it's my birthday!"

"And me, and me, I'm four, too. Have you got me a present?"

While Scott reprimanded the boys for their lack of manners, Michelle explained the 'Uncle Wally' thing.

Apparently, Scott calls Oliver Olly, which the boys struggled to say when they were small, so they call him Wally. It was difficult to keep a straight face, and Oliver gave me a fake stern look.

"Boys, this is Oliver's friend Hannah, come and say hello," Scott said.

Kent said hello and shook my hand, but Ricky just stared at me and said, "I like the pink bits in your hair. Mummy, can I have pink in my hair? Are you Uncle Wally's girlfriend, Hannah?" And, much to my amazement, he climbed onto my lap.

I was lost for words again, but Scott rescued the situation beautifully. "Hannah is Uncle Wally's friend and she's a girl, so yes, you could say that, I think," and he grinned at me. "If you stay still for two minutes, I think Uncle Wally and Hannah have something for you both."

The presents were well received, and the twins went off to play on the slide their grandparents had bought them for their birthday. The adults remained on the patio, and the afternoon flew by with good-natured teasing and a lot of laughter. Around four o'clock, Michelle asked if Sylvia and I would help bring out the food for the afternoon tea they had prepared. I was surprised how comfortable I felt with this family and was enjoying myself. As we laid the table in the garden, Oliver gave me the raised eyebrows look, which I read as 'Are you okay?' I nodded and smiled. He was looking out for me without fussing, which made me think what a good man he was.

We had sandwiches, quiche and a fabulous salad with

cold meats, finger food for the twins, followed by birthday cake, with champagne for the adults. Scott and Michelle were great hosts, and it was an enjoyable day. After we had eaten, Oliver, Scott and Jack insisted on clearing away and loading the dishwasher while Michelle, Sylvia and I relaxed and played with the twins.

"Why do you have two names, Hannah? Uncle Wally calls you Freddie, that's a boy's name." That came from Ricky, who seemed the most inquisitive of the twins. I explained the situation as simply as I could for a four-year-old, and Sylvia and Michelle were laughing.

"Mummy said it's time Uncle Wally got married. Are you going to marry Uncle Wally?" was the next question. Michelle tried to distract him with the puzzle but to no avail.

I took a deep breath. I have always believed it's best to be as honest as you can be with children in a way they can understand. "Well, I was married before I met Uncle Wally, and I wasn't very good at it. So, I don't think I want to try again. Anyway, Your Uncle Wally might not want to get married, or maybe not to me," was the best I could manage.

"That's silly. Daddy says when I'm trying to do a puzzle that I will only be good at something if I keep trying until I get it right. So, you need to keep trying at being married until you are good at it. Uncle Wally will help you, won't you, Uncle Wally?" I had no idea the men had finished in the kitchen and were standing behind us. I could feel my cheeks burning.

"Nothing like a child for telling it like it is! Sorry, Hannah," said Scott. "Come on, you two, say goodnight to Hannah, Uncle Wally, Grandma and Grampy and Mummy. It's time for your bath." After a few feeble attempts to delay the inevitable, the twins hugged everyone and followed their dad indoors.

Diplomatically, the others moved the conversation on to other topics. As the sun set, Oliver suggested calling a taxi and collecting his car the next day, as we had had a few drinks. We went back to mine, made some tea and cheese on toast and went over the day.

"I knew they'd love you, the only problem is, if we did ever get married, we'd have to let Ricky be a bridesmaid with pink hair." Oliver's humour completely defused what had been the elephant in the room. We were still laughing when we went to bed.

When I woke the next morning, there was a cup of lukewarm coffee by the bed and a note which read, 'Missing you already, gone to collect my car and go to work. Talk to you later xxx'

Deal Or No Deal

So, I was in a relationship, it seemed. How the heck did this happen? I mean, I was practically a founder member of the Oliver fan club, having been obsessed with him for as long as I can remember, but I had sworn an oath to singledom, remember? My dilemma: risk another disastrous break up and all that it entails, or put an end to this nonsense before it gets out of hand? On the plus side, my previous history of disastrous break ups inevitably led to some serious weight loss, which I felt was a good thing. Fortunately, I have never been a comfort eater when I'm miserable, but my friends think I'm a bit obsessive regarding my weight. Flashback to my marriage to Charles (Laboutins), when I was seductively lying on the sofa, with his head on my lap and he asked if it bothered me that my "tummy was all squashy?" I spent weeks doing stomach crunches and leg raises until my stomach resembled an ironing board and I was unable to laugh because my muscles were so painful.

I digress, back to the matter at hand. Throw in the towel and admit I was heading into the unknown with a man who seemed almost too good to be true? Do the whole 'go with the flow' thing and hope I didn't end up with another broken string to my bow? Or walk away and forever wonder what could have been? I felt like I was on an episode of *Deal Or No Deal* and I was left with two boxes: £1 or £500,000. The more I thought about the situation, the more my brain felt like the M25 in rush-hour traffic with roadworks everywhere. There was only one way to clear my head: I went shopping.

By the time I got home, my credit card was almost in tears from the beating it had taken. My feet were sore, my arms felt six inches longer and my brain still felt like a washing machine on a fast spin cycle. I made some coffee and plonked myself on the sofa, surrounded by the bags of therapy. I was no further forward in my dilemma, and several hundred pounds poorer, and I couldn't remember most of what I had bought.

There were many signs that were pointing me in the right direction with my relationship with Oliver, but I was either too stubborn or too scared to see them. The turning point was a mini break in Rome that Oliver had booked as a surprise for me as a pre-birthday treat. I'm a huge fan of all things Italian: pizza, pasta, gelato, handbags and shoes. I'm not big on flying but needs must and all that.

The trip would later be described by my mother as 'a catalogue of disasters', 'a comedy of errors' and '*The Shit Show* starring Hannah Matthews'.

If ever there were any doubt about Oliver's patience, I can safely tell you, this man is the most tolerant, patient, understanding man I know. He probably has a saint named after him, and rightly so, in my opinion. We arrived at the airport by taxi, which dropped us at the entrance and drove away with my handbag still on the back seat. Not the end of the world, Oliver phoned the taxi company, and the driver returned in less than ten minutes. So, another twenty quid to him for his trouble, thanks Oliver. After confirming my passport and credit cards were inside, we progressed to check-in. No problems there. My suitcase was under the maximum weight by about two grams.

We decided to go through security straight away and find a nice bar to relax and await our flight. After some raised eyebrows over the quantity of liquids allowed in hand luggage, Oliver kindly grabbed another of those teeny-weeny plastic bags and took my face cream and other lotions and potions as his liquids so that disaster was averted. Do these people not understand how important skincare is? And doesn't Oliver have face cream of his own? After struggling back into my jacket, scarf, belt and heels, we headed for the duty free via the escalators. After my boarding pass flew out of my hand, Oliver managed to catch it before it fell through a crack, but as I turned to take it and thank him, my stupid heel got caught in the little ridge in the escalator. As we reached the bottom, I managed to get the shoe free, but unfortunately, the heel was no longer part of the shoe, which, in turn, jammed the escalator and caused some muttering and grumbling from other passengers. My face was as red as my heel-less shoe, but Oliver was laughing, not unkindly, which made me see the funny side, too.

We went to one of the shops and bought me a cheap pair

of flip-flops for the journey, and Oliver was still laughing as he said, "Well, Freddie, I was hoping we'd have some great adventures together and maybe a little shopping, but I wasn't expecting it to all happen before we've left the country!"

We chose a bar and sat watching the world go by while we waited for our flight. No drama there, unless you count me opening a packet of crisps that flew all over the place and knocking over my drink in my subsequent fluster. Good job it was not red wine, I suppose. The man at the next table had been behind us on the escalator. "Hope you guys have holiday insurance, she's an accident looking for somewhere to happen, mate," he laughed. We smiled and left the bar, hoping he wasn't on our flight.

We boarded without any issues and had a comfortable flight to Rome. We took a taxi to our hotel and, although he didn't say anything, I noticed Oliver checking I had my handbag this time. After checking in, we went up to our room to unpack and have a quick shower before going out to dinner. Our room, while quite small, was beautifully decorated in blues and golds with a bathroom to match. Weirdly, the bathroom was the bigger of the two rooms, with a sunken bath, a huge walk-in shower and double sinks. I decided that the bath looked too good to miss, so when Oliver suggested a quick shower and maybe catching the second half of some football game in the bar before dinner, I happily opted for a soak while he went to the bar. I poured in some of the luxury bubble bath and started the bath running, sorted out my hair and make-up products and called my friend Louisa. After ten minutes of hysterical laughing at my series of unfortunate events on the journey so far, I switched to video call to show her the room. "Honestly, Louisa, it's beautiful, isn't it? And look at the luxury bathroom! Oh crap! What the heck? Gotta go and sort this mess, bye!" The bubbles were at least two feet tall and just about to pour onto the floor, so getting into the bath was clearly not an option. I pulled out the plug, tied back my hair and jumped in the shower. By the time I got out, the water in the bath had drained away, but the bubbles had not. It looked like someone had made a giant meringue in there. And, right on cue, Oliver made his entrance.

"Hey, Freddie, have you drowned in there? You've been ages! Can I come in?"

I must have said yes, as the next second Oliver was in the bathroom staring at the tub. "Are you in there? What on earth happened? Are you okay?" He started poking at the bubbles with his finger.

"I'm here, and I'm fine, apart from overdoing the bubble bath. I was on the phone to Louisa, and I wasn't paying attention to it. I'm sorry, I'm such an idiot!" I mumbled from behind the door.

Oliver's reaction was not what I expected. "No harm done, you get dressed while I try and clear this a bit and we'll go and get some lovely Italian food, shall we?" And he gave me a hug. I sheepishly got dressed while he ran the cold tap and tried to swish the bubbles away.

We had a fantastic meal in a small restaurant about a

ten-minute walk from the hotel, a very nice bottle of wine and Oliver produced a possible itinerary of things to see and do over the next few days. We agreed on all the usual tourist attractions, looked at opening times and worked out the best way to see everything without exhausting ourselves. It seemed that Oliver had done his homework; the only thing we hadn't thought about (well, I hadn't thought about) was the amount of walking involved. Of course, I had brought three pairs of heels, two pairs of strappy sandals, the flip-flops from the airport, and one pair of trainers that, although at least three years old, had never graced my feet. I'm not really a trainers type of girl. I mean, they're okay if that's your thing, but they look weird on me.

The next morning dawned bright, sunny and pleasantly warm. After a light breakfast, and wearing the lovely trainers, we set off for the Colosseum. Oliver had pre-booked and opted for a guided tour, as opposed to the headphones, and it was fascinating. Oliver was enthralled, but I found it a little depressing thinking of all the people that had lost their lives there. We covered the Roman Forum and Palatine Hill and had a very educational morning. I realised I was very hungry; all the walking had given me an appetite, so we found a street food vendor and ordered *pizza al taglio* and *supplì*, delicious little rice balls filled with mozzarella and covered in tomato sauce. Oliver pored over the map on his phone for a while, had a conversation in what can only be described as Italglish with the street vendor and, before I knew what was going on, we were at the taxi rank. The taxi, surprisingly quickly, dropped us at a shopping centre and, as Oliver paid the driver, he grinned at me.

"You're limping already, I suspect you have blisters, so I think some sensible footwear is called for. No arguments, Freddie, plasters and new shoes. Let's go." I already had plasters in my bag, so we headed for a very expensive-looking shop a few metres away. Oliver picked some shoes that I can only describe as 'practical' and I tried them, trying not to look horrified at a) the price and b) how ugly they were. Though it kills me to admit it, they were the softest, most comfortable things my feet had ever encountered.

Oliver was doing his utmost not to laugh at my expression and failing. "Maybe a different colour?" He pointed at the shoes and asked the sales assistant, "*Rosa? L'azzuro?*"

"*No, solo giallo.*" So, I end up with the ugliest bright yellow shoes you can imagine, and Oliver was nearly 200 euros poorer.

Our first argument was about the shoes. "I'll get these for you, Freddie." Oliver had his credit card out ready.

"My blisters were self-inflicted down to my vanity and I'm the one who has to wear them, so I'm paying and that's that."

"I chose Rome and it's my fault you have walked for miles. Why would you buy something you hate? I, on the other hand, love them. They're very stylish and they suit you. And you don't have your purse with you, it's still in the safe at the hotel, so…?"

At this point, the decision was taken out of my hands.

Although I insisted on paying him back, Oliver wouldn't hear of it. We argued back and forth until I gave in.

"So, thank you, Oliver, I will treasure them always, and wear them at every available opportunity."

We left the shop giggling like kids, with Oliver stopping every few yards to point at the shoes and say loudly, "Wow, Freddie, what lovely shoes you're wearing today," and laughing again.

The rest of the afternoon passed in a blur of sightseeing, people watching and chatting. Although I felt incredibly self-conscious in the yellow shoes, they were so comfortable I eventually got over my embarrassment and got on with enjoying the day. We hadn't planned a venue for dinner, so it was a mutual decision to eat in the hotel restaurant, partly to give my blisters a break, and partly because they had a live band due to play and a large dance floor. The food was delicious. I had a prawn and asparagus risotto, and Oliver chose a seafood linguine. After drinking rather more wine than I was used to, and several liqueurs, we hit the dance floor. Vanity had overtaken comfort, and I was wearing my favourite strappy high heels, so dancing would have been difficult had I not been slightly inebriated. As it was, I threw caution to the wind and was doing a fantastic impression of an epileptic octopus when I spun round with my arms flailing and managed to punch Oliver squarely in the face. In an instant, I was stone cold sober and absolutely mortified. Oliver's lip was bleeding, so I reached over to the table to grab a napkin, apologising profusely. Inevitably, I managed to knock over a glass of water in my haste, which emptied onto the tablecloth, rolled onto the floor and smashed. That expression 'wanting the ground to open up' was never more appropriate, but good old Oliver was laughing.

I, on the other hand, was close to tears. "I'm so, so sorry, I'm such an idiot, are you okay? Of course you're not okay, your lip is bleeding. You must think I'm such a klutz. Well I am, I know."

Oliver guided me away from the broken glass as the waiter discreetly slipped behind me to clean up the mess. He took my hand, still smiling. "Freddie, stop stressing, it was an accident and I'm fine. You are a klutz, but you're the sweetest, funniest, most beautiful klutz I ever met, and I love you. Let's go up to our room before you get us arrested for criminal damage or you accidentally assault someone else." I almost missed the 'I love you' bit, and I did wonder if I had misheard him, so I said nothing, and we went up to our room.

I woke around five thirty the next morning with a raging thirst and a woodpecker inside my head. I slipped quietly out of bed and found some paracetamol and a can of Pepsi, which I downed in seconds. I sat in a chair by the window for a while, waiting for the sun to wake up, going over the previous evening in my head. Had Oliver really said he loved me? Was it just the alcohol talking? Was it a throwaway remark or a genuine statement? How did I feel about him? Should I bring the subject up with him now we were both sober? Should I just forget about it? My head was back on fast spin in the washing machine syndrome, although the paracetamol had subdued the woodpecker a level.

Oliver's phone vibrating stirred him. He sat up, looking bemused and grinned at me as he reached for the phone. "It is six thirty in the morning in Italy, bud, what's up?" The grin turned into a grimace. Oliver was silent, listening intently for a few minutes. "Crap, I'm so sorry. We'll get a flight straight back, okay? Keep me posted. I'll keep my phone on until the flight. Try not to worry, did you call Mum and Dad? Of course, they're away too, damn. I'll call you as soon as I've sorted a flight, take it easy, speak later."

I had no idea what was going on, but I knew it was serious by Oliver's tone, so I was already grabbing our cases and emptying the wardrobe. "What's happened, Oliver?"

"Kent is really unwell; they have no idea what's wrong, but they called the out of hours GP who are sending an ambulance. It sounds awful. We need to get back as soon as possible. My parents are away in South Africa at their holiday home, so…" He tailed off and I could see he was struggling to hold it together.

"Right, if you sort out flights, I'll pack for us both and let the hotel know we're leaving and why. We need to get dressed then I'll pack everything else. Try not to worry, we will get there as soon as we can." I instinctively hugged him. He hugged me back so tightly I could hardly breathe.

Is This Love?

The next two hours were manic, but at the same time surprisingly calm. By eight-thirty we were in a taxi, on the way to the airport. I have no idea how we managed it, but someone was looking out for us up there, and by eleven-thirty we were in the air. Oliver had called Scott from the airport but the only thing he knew was Kent was undergoing loads of tests. I could see Oliver was really agitated on the flight but trying to remain calm. I took his hand. "Oliver, I understand you're worried sick and rightly so. Try to be positive. Worrying yourself silly isn't going to help you. Kent is a healthy, beautiful child, in the best possible place, the hospital has a reputation for the best paediatric care and, for now, all we can do is hope he'll be okay, or pray, or whatever we feel will help. There's nothing we can do at this moment, and we need to stay strong for Scott and Michelle. They'll need people who are positive and optimistic to support them through this. And I'll do whatever I can to support you."

"Freddie, thank you. If that's your 'man-up' speech, it's working. I'm so grateful to have you by my side and I hope I always will." He gave me a half-hearted grin.

We landed, were first off the plane thanks to the

amazing crew and, after grabbing our bags, we got a taxi straight to the hospital. We looked a right pair of weirdos, trailing our cases behind us, me in the infamous yellow shoes. We were shown to a side room by a nurse, she called it the family room, to wait.

After a few minutes, Michelle came into the room. "Thank you for coming, Kent has meningitis." She promptly burst into tears.

As I hugged her, I shook my head at Oliver, who I could see was about to start questioning her. He picked up my meaning straight away, and simply said, "What can we do to help?"

Michelle gradually regained her composure. "I'm sure you want to see him, Scott is in there, but only two people are allowed at a time. I'll take you in and Scott can explain better than me what's going on. My other concern is, of course, Ricky. We had to leave him with our neighbour who is nearly eighty but there was no one else to ask." And she started to cry again.

"If you give me a key to your house, I'll take our cases and get over there, collect Ricky and take care of him. No arguments, you all need to be here with Kent for the moment. It's the sensible solution. I know he doesn't know me well but I'm sure we'll be okay."

Oliver immediately agreed, although Michelle said it was a lot to ask.

"You didn't ask, I offered," I said with a smile. And so, after a quick peek at Kent, who was sleeping, Oliver helped me to a taxi with all our bags.

I managed to take the bags in, with the help of the taxi driver, and made myself a strong coffee before going next door to collect Ricky. I suddenly felt quite weak and realised we had not eaten at all that day, so I raided the biscuit tin, too. Michelle had phoned the neighbour to tell her I would collect Ricky and to let him know what would be happening.

To his credit, and my relief, he was delighted to see me. "This is my nearly-auntie Hannah," he told the neighbour.

I blushed and she smiled. "How is Kent doing? And Michelle and Scott?" she asked.

"I don't know much. Kent has meningitis but he's doing okay as far as they can say. I'm going to look after Ricky until, well, while I'm needed."

"I was sad my brother is poorly, so Mrs Mac helped me make some brownies to cheer me up," Ricky announced. "She said we can take them home 'cos she can't have them 'cos she has dyer beets."

Mrs Mac laughed. "I do have diabetes, and I did say he could take them home, but I also told him they're only for after dinner and he should only have one, and how important it is to brush your teeth properly afterwards." Mrs Mac had obviously had children and was a wise woman. I, on the other hand, have not, and it would seem lack of experience leaves one vulnerable to their ploys to get what they want.

There was a long list. "Mummy always gives me ice cream when I'm sad. Daddy says only little girls have to eat vegetables; boys can have chips. Uncle Wally says I'm big now, so I can go to bed whenever I want." Suffice to say, dinner was chicken dinosaurs with chips and alphabet spaghetti (that took a while with having to make everyone's name out of the letters), ice cream for dessert, and bedtime was when his eyes started to close, which thankfully was half an hour before mine. I decided it was prudent to sleep in the twins' room, but on cushions on the floor, as it didn't feel right to sleep in Kent's bed.

Oliver texted as I was getting settled. 'Kent stable, no real improvement but no worse. Be back in the morning, thank you, love you xxx'.

While I was wondering whether to pretend I was already asleep, my fingers made their own decision.

'That's good news. Get some rest, you too xxx'. I was exhausted and thought I would sleep right through.

2am: "Hannah, can I wake you up if I need anything?"

"Of course you can, poppet, what do you need?"

"Nothing. I just wanted to know."

3.12am: "Hannah, I need a wee." Dealt with appropriately.

4.45am: "Hannah, is Kent going to die? Raffy's grandma went to hospital, and she died." This one took a little longer to deal with, but he seemed reassured and finally we both went back to sleep.

6.20am: "Hannah, shall we do a jigsaw puzzle? That's what me and Kent do when it's too early to wake up Mummy and Daddy." The benefits of strong black coffee came into their own and we were still sitting on the bedroom floor doing puzzles when Scott and Oliver came in. The plan for the next twenty-four hours was put into place.

Oliver on Ricky duty from 8am-1pm, while Scott slept and I went home to unpack and shower. Scott at the hospital for the afternoon while Michelle came back to the house to sleep. I return at 1.30pm and Oliver sleeps while I take care of Ricky. Scott and Michelle at the hospital overnight while Oliver and I take care of Ricky.

After a few days of us playing musical babysitters, Kent was making great progress, so Michelle and Scott took turns staying at the hospital so one of them was home with Ricky. Oliver and I helped as much as we could, although Oliver had gone back to work. I worked mornings for a week, so I could take Ricky out to the adventure playground or the museum to see the dinosaurs.

Another New Beginning

When Kent was discharged, he seemed back to normal quite quickly but had to have regular check-ups to make sure all was well. Oliver's parents were now back from their trip to South Africa and were spending their time helping out with the boys, too. Michelle seemed to be struggling to get back to normal. She was pale and looking tired most of the time. She had also lost weight. Although I was seeing them on a regular basis with Oliver, and we babysat on occasion, I didn't feel it was my place to talk to Michelle about my concerns, for fear of overstepping the mark. It was Sylvia who brought it up when Oliver and I were with his parents for Sunday lunch.

"Have you noticed how tired Michelle is looking, Hannah? Between you and me, I'm concerned about her but don't want to be an interfering mother-in-law. What do you think we should do? Maybe you could talk to her? Or is that asking too much?"

I was quite pleased to be asked. "I have been thinking the same but was worried about speaking out of turn. If you think it's okay, I will, we're seeing them on Wednesday, taking the boys out for pizza."

"Hannah, you are practically family, your opinions are

always welcome, and I know Michelle and Scott feel the same." Sylvia patted my hand.

The following week, Oliver and I picked the twins up from school, and took them out for the promised pizza. When we took them back, I suggested Oliver help Scott to bath them and, fortunately, they took the bait.

"Michelle, feel free to tell me to mind my own business but I'm concerned about you, and so is Sylvia. You look tired and you've lost weight. Is there anything we can help with?"

Michelle smiled. "I'm concerned, too, and yes, I'm hoping you'll be able to help me. There's going to be an addition to the family in November." She was grinning like a lunatic now, but it took a minute for me to catch on. She continued, "We were planning on telling everyone next weekend, when I'm at twelve weeks, but it seems we've been rumbled. We'll tell Oliver when the twins are in bed, and I'll call Sylvia tomorrow. We won't tell the boys until nearer the time, obviously. Do I look that bad that you thought I was ill?" I nodded and we were both laughing when the boys came down with their dad and Uncle Wally to say goodnight.

A few weeks later, and after the family had all been told the news, Oliver and I met up for dinner at Seafood and Eat in town. And yes, we do eat out far too frequently for our waistlines and my budget. On this occasion, it was a celebration as, on top of the baby news, Oliver had been offered a promotion at work. It was a substantial rise in pay, which was always a good thing, but also a change in hours with hardly any night shifts compared to what he was used to. We were both pleased about that. We both started to speak at the same time and laughed.

"You first, Freddie," he said.

"Okay. I'm planning to take my mum to the US for a ten-day visit. She has a close friend there called Betty who she hasn't seen in years and she's apprehensive about travelling on her own, so I've offered to go with her. Betty's husband died a year ago, and she's not in great health herself. I thought it would be nice for her to see Mum. And vice versa. Would it be cheeky to ask you to take care of my place while I'm away? I mean, you don't need to stay there, although you can if you'd like, just stop by, water the plants, check the post and stuff like that. What's so funny Oliver?" He was grinning like a loon.

"So, what I was about to ask, even more cheekily, was if I could stay at yours for a couple of weeks? My landlord has put the place on the market, and I've been dragging my heels about whether it's the right time to buy. Well, a buyer has materialised for the landlord very quickly and they're in a hurry, so I'm in a bit of a spot. I could stay with Scott and Michelle, but they are already tight for space, and my parents' place is too far from work." He tailed off, looking sheepish.

"Oliver, I think we have a deal. We spend most of our free time together, anyway, stay at mine for as long as you need to."

Mum and I had an amazing time in America. Betty lived in Florida, not in a touristy place but a little town on the edge of what was then the Gulf of Mexico, now called the Gulf of America. I did a little exploring, and a lot of shopping, while Mum and Betty sat on the lanai by the pool, catching up on each other's lives, and reminiscing about their early years when they both lived and worked in England. I loved the weather, and the fact I could swim every afternoon, and we went out to eat every other day, so Betty didn't feel she had to cook for us all the time. Oliver and I texted or spoke on the phone every day and were both surprised how much we missed one another. When we left, both Mum and Betty cried, believing it unlikely they would ever see one another again and I found myself promising I would try to get Mum back again the following year.

We had an overnight flight back from Tampa to Gatwick, and Oliver was waiting for us in arrivals. He made a big fuss of my mum, insisting on taking both our cases and asked a thousand questions about the trip. We took Mum home first. Oliver had bought milk and bread for her and had brought a small dish of lasagne he had made so she would be able to rest and not have to worry about shopping. Mum was very grateful and when she said, "Hannah, this young man is what you youngsters call a keeper. I'd advise you to hang on to him," I was mortified.

Oliver, of course, thought it was hilarious. After we left Mum's, he was saying, "Your mother, Freddie, is a very wise woman. She knows a good thing when she sees it. I think you should take her advice and keep me." As is so rarely the case, I was speechless but secretly agreed.

Is This My Happy Ending?

Six weeks later, Oliver was still living at my house, and we were getting on famously. No relationship is perfect, and we had the odd disagreement here and there, but it never amounted to anything we couldn't talk about, and compromise on. We went house hunting together, and I soon realised he was looking for something that would work for us as a couple, as opposed to a house for him alone. I sat down with him over breakfast one morning and took a deep breath.

"Where are we going with this, Oliver? It seems we are drifting into the future without a real direction and I'm not sure how I feel about that. I mean, we're viewing houses like we are planning on living together properly, but we haven't really talked it through. Where do you see this going? I can't afford two mortgages, and I'm confused."

"Okay, my darling Freddie. You have a point, and I should have been more open with you, but in all honesty, I've been hoping you'd just go with the flow. I've been scared to ask in case you say an outright no. I love you; I'd be over the moon if we bought something together, but I'm worried about rushing you. My dream is a future with you, with our children playing in the garden and you as my wife. I'll work my socks off to give you the best life I can, you can have as many shoes as we can afford. This is clumsy, and not how I'd planned it, but, my beautiful, funny, kind and wonderful Freddie, will you marry me?"

The tears were streaming down my face, and I knew in that moment that I'd happily be barefoot for the rest of my life to spend it with Oliver. I managed to nod and blubbed, "Yes, yes please. Oliver… the bacon's on fire!" We both leapt up, I grabbed the pan from under the grill and threw it in the sink as Oliver grabbed a tea towel to diffuse the smoke and opened the back door.

"I knew from the moment we set off for Italy that life with you would never be dull, Freddie. I haven't stopped laughing since we got together. I think, together we can set the whole world on fire. In the meantime, let's go out for breakfast."

We waited until Scott and Michelle's beautiful daughter Cassidy had arrived safely before getting married in a quiet and beautifully simple ceremony at the majestic Manor Hotel four days before Christmas. The guest list was small – both our immediate families and a handful of friends – but it was a beautiful day. Although chilly, it was crisp and bright, and certainly the happiest day of my life. Oliver looked beyond handsome in a charcoal-grey suit with a dark grey and silver striped tie. I wore a simple red silk sheath dress and stunning silver shoes with a soft silvery grey pashmina. The silver shoes were a bit Yanni style; in fact, he had come with me to choose them. Strappy and sparkly with enough of a heel to look elegant but substantial enough to withstand my dancing. I had tested them out to Abba's 'Dancing Queen' at home in my PJs without breaking an ankle, so I felt confident on the day. My hair, under strict orders from the hairdresser, behaved impeccably, as did Kent and Ricky as page boys. We were joined for the evening by the wider family and more friends and colleagues from work and it was quite a lively evening. The band Oliver had arranged were setting up and, as we got up for our first dance, I realised we had not planned or even discussed what the song would be. Oliver went over to the stage and was handed a microphone.

"As most of you will know, my beautiful wife Hannah is affectionately known as Freddie. I'm hoping she will be okay with me explaining why." He looked over at me with that sexy, raised eyebrow look he does so well. I rolled my eyes, laughing, and nodded. He told the story perfectly, and the band struck up with Queen's 'Don't Stop Me Now'. Our guests roared with laughter and clapped and cheered as we took to the dance floor.

Christmas, I was hoping, would be a quiet, relaxed affair after all the hustle and bustle of the wedding, but that was not how things panned out at all. Both families gathered at Sylvia and Jack's, including my mum and my sister, so there were twelve of us in all. It was loud, messy and manic but one of the best Christmases I can remember. Mum and Sylvia had bonded like sisters, and made me think of army captains, organising the food, the games and the clearing up. It was such a good day, even Kent throwing up on my lap after too much trifle couldn't dampen my spirits. Boxing Day was a rerun of Christmas Day, but with cold meats and salads, and Kent was fully recovered, thankfully.

We had decided on a February honeymoon, and my amazing husband had suggested Florida, so we could take Mum to Betty's again. We stayed in a hotel after leaving Mum and Betty to a fortnight of talking each other to death. I won't bore you with the details, that's too much information and we'd all be embarrassed, but the honeymoon was everything you would expect and more. The weather was perfect, not too hot but wall-to-wall sunshine, the food was delicious and Oliver was gorgeous, of course. After making memories to last a lifetime, we picked up my mum, and after a tearful farewell lunch with Betty, we headed home.

We settled quickly in our new home, not far from Scott and Michelle's, and got back to normal life: work, eat, sleep and repeat. We were both working hard, having work done in the house and planning for the future. We had decided to wait only a few months to try for a baby, partly because we weren't exactly spring chickens, but we wanted the house to be completed first. The kitchen was the biggest job and seemed to be taking forever. I found myself getting stressed out daily. I had an important work meeting one morning and couldn't find my car keys. With hindsight, I was perhaps a little grumpy.

"Oliver! Have you seen my car keys? I'm sure I left them in what remains of this disaster area that should be a kitchen by now. Oliver?" I was shouting.

"If you weren't so flipping untidy, and you put things where they live, you wouldn't lose things on an hourly basis, Hannah!" Oliver only ever called me Hannah when he was annoyed.

I was furious. "So says the slob who can't even manage to put the lid on the toothpaste and his underwear in the laundry basket. I'm going to be late now, if you know where the keys are, just tell me and stop being a dick!" I'm not nice when I'm angry.

Oliver strutted over to the key rack in the hall, lifted my keys and handed them to me without a word. I marched out and slammed the door behind me. When I arrived at the office, I discovered the meeting had, in fact, been postponed and the office admin had emailed me that morning to let me know. Obviously, I hadn't checked my emails. This was not turning into a good day. I drove home in a foul mood, angry at myself for not being on the ball, and still furious with Oliver, who I could see later didn't deserve to be on the receiving end of my temper due to my own lack of organisational ability.

When I got home, Oliver looked concerned. "Are you okay, Freddie? Not like you to fly off the handle like that. And for the record, I'm sorry I put your keys on the hook without telling you, and I'm sorry I'm a slob. I'll make us a coffee." Honestly, this man is pure gold, and I don't deserve him.

"I'm sorry, too, and you have nothing to apologise for, Oliver, you are not a slob but I'm an absolute bitch." And I burst into tears.

Oliver stopped what he was doing to hug me. "Freddie, you're not a bitch at all. You are stressed over the house and the chaos we're living in, and I should be more helpful and understanding." He carried on making the coffee.

I sat myself at the breakfast bar, feeling even worse than I had, knowing I had been so awful, and Oliver was being so nice about it. He put some of my favourite chocolate digestives in front of me, smiling. I smiled back and started on the first of about five of them.

"Any left?" Oliver joked as he slid the coffee towards me. I suddenly realised I was going to throw up, leapt off the stool and ran for the bathroom. Oliver gave me a couple of minutes and tapped gingerly on the door. "I'm coming in, Freddie, is that okay?" He handed me a cold, wet flannel to wipe my face, and an ice cube to suck. My expression was puzzled. "My darling girl, I have a feeling we may be pregnant. I remember Michelle being sick every time she smelled coffee when she was having the twins."

"I… We… Do you… Can we… My God, really? Are you sure?" I was in total shock and barely able to string a sentence together.

"Well, we need to do a test, obviously. But you have been a little bit weird lately. I mean you're always weird, but in a good way. You've certainly been a bit unpredictable, and perhaps, if I may say so, not your normal sunny self. Borderline grumpy, to be truthful. But I still love you, and it would certainly explain things. Oh no, I'm sorry, I didn't mean to make you cry."

"I'm crying because I'm happy, I think. And scared, and

shocked, and excited, and scared again. To be honest, I'm bloody terrified, Oliver, what if I am pregnant and I can't do it? What if I'm a terrible mother?"

Oliver grinned at me and squeezed my hand. "Well, at least our kid will have one awesome parent if you're rubbish at it, that's more than some kids have. Seriously, Freddie, listen to yourself. Kent and Ricky adore you, and you're amazing with them. Remember when Kent was so ill, you had zero experience, but you cared for Ricky like you were born to it? Cassidy already loves you, who wouldn't? And I will be with you every step of the way, I promise. Let's go and get a test, but I'm 99% certain we're pregnant."

No one likes a smart-arse, but on this occasion, I let that go. We decided to keep it to ourselves for a few weeks to get past the first twelve weeks and get the kitchen finished, but I was rumbled, first by Michelle and Sylvia when I turned down a glass of wine.

"Hannah, you have either had a personality transplant, you're a body double pretending to be Hannah, or you're pregnant… OMG you are pregnant, I'm so excited for you both!" Michelle was dancing round the kitchen, laughing. I realised I needed to tell my family before the news spread like wildfire, but my own mother is borderline psychic. As soon as she opened the front door, she hugged me, then pushed me away at arm's length and studied my face closely. "Well. I'm thinking you're here to tell me I'm going to be a grandma," she said with raised eyebrows. And again, I burst into tears.

She made a cup of tea, which was bearable, and we sat together on the sofa. "I have never lied to you, Hannah, and that won't change. Having a baby is difficult for many people, it is indeed painful. But the end result is so incredible, there is not a feeling on earth to match seeing your own child for the first time. I thought my heart would burst right out of my chest with each of you. I promise you, it will bring you happiness you can't even imagine. You also are blessed to have Oliver, who I think will continue to be an amazing support to you, and a doting father, I have no doubt about that. Try and relax and enjoy the pregnancy. You have always known you wanted to be a mother, and I know you'll be amazing. You have an army of people who will help or advise where needed, and don't be afraid to ask for help. Is there anything you want to ask me?"

"Do you happen to have a tin of pilchards? I would love pilchards on toast, please." What on earth was happening to me?

After a couple of weeks, I was feeling a little more chilled. Thousands of women have babies every day and they do it more than once, so it can't be that bad. By the time my scan date came round, I was feeling upbeat and excited. We had agreed on not knowing the sex of the baby until he or she was born, which is often not known at twelve weeks apparently, but we had picked names. Jackson for a boy, and Eva or Olivia for a girl. The sonographer was lovely, very friendly, and I was completely relaxed until she smiled and asked, "Any history of twins in the family? We have two little people in here. Congratulations!" Yet again, I burst into tears.

To his credit, Oliver managed to keep a lid on his excitement to calm me down. I was sobbing, absolutely terrified. I wasn't sure I was ready for one baby, never mind two at once. The sonographer was very understanding; my reaction was quite normal, apparently.

The journey home was mostly in silence. Oliver reached over and patted my leg once or twice, and he asked if I was okay. I shrugged, too numb to speak. After we had eaten, I sat on the sofa, staring blankly at nothing. Oliver reached out for my hand.

"Freddie, we are having twins. It's happening, and it's a fact. I understand it's a big shock, but we are very, very lucky and we need to look at this as a positive step. I know Michelle felt the same initially but look at them now. We have a loving family that will help us wherever they can, we've got this. I give you my solemn promise that I will love you and support you, I'll be there for you and the twins, every step of the way. Together, we can take on the world, and this is only two kids!" I couldn't help but smile. Somehow, Oliver always had the right words to reassure me. So, I put on my 'big girl pants', which I needed after a few more weeks, and got on with the business of being pregnant.

Changes

Both our families were delighted. Of course they were, they weren't the ones having twins. They were also very supportive, particularly Michelle, who obviously knew exactly how I was feeling. We had decided that I would stop work and take on the role of consultant, enabling me to work as and when I felt I could manage it, so I was mostly at home doing occasional days' work for the company I had been employed by. I spent my free time either with Oliver when he wasn't working, Mum, or Michelle, who would come over with Cassidy while the boys were at school. We were trying not to refer to them as 'the twins' anymore, to avoid confusion when there were two sets.

Typically, I was sick more than I was not, and Oliver seemed to be coming out in sympathy. As I got bigger, he seemed to get smaller. I had noticed over several weeks that he'd lost weight and was frequently more tired than usual. He put it down to work stress, but after one particularly heated discussion when he kept saying, "Stop worrying about me, Freddie, I'm fine. Let's focus on you and the babies," I got angry with him.

"You don't look fine, you're always tired and you're

clearly not eating enough. The last thing I need is a sick husband to take care of right now, so you had better get yourself to the doctor, and soon."

As soon as the words left my mouth, I felt sick. What if he was really ill, and I was being so selfish and nasty? Tears again, what was wrong with me?

"Oliver, I'm so sorry, I didn't mean that. I love you more than anything in the world and I'm worried about you. Of course I would look after you, no matter what. You know that, don't you? Please forgive me."

Oliver stood up and put his arms around me. "Of course I forgive you, you silly goose. You're right, though, you don't need me being ill, you have more than enough on your plate. I promise I'll call the doctor in the morning and find out what is making me feel like crap. Hey, you don't think I might be pregnant too, do you? On the plus side, we'd be overnight millionaires!" He was my Oliver again, grinning like a loon.

"I'll come with you to the doctor, if you'd like. I suspect he will tell me I'm married to an idiot, but it would be good to have that confirmed by a professional. Shall I make us some drinking chocolate, and we could have an early night?" I suggested, smiling.

He was laughing now. "Great idea!" He winked at me. "At least we don't have to worry about you getting pregnant."

Four days later, we sat in the doctor's office. He was a kindly older man, who seemed to have all the time in the world for us. He listened intently to Oliver's brief outline of what was going on, then turned to me with a smile. "What are your thoughts? Men sometimes tend to play down their symptoms and will only come to see a doctor when their wife has nagged them into it. I mean no offence, of course, but I can see by your expression I may have hit the nail on the head. Am I right?"

"Actually, that's exactly it. I've been nagging for a while, and Oliver has lost more than a few pounds, close to a stone, I think. And he does work hard, I know, but his tiredness is more than tiredness, if that makes sense, it's worrying me. Thank you for listening."

"So, we'll get you booked in for some blood tests first of all, Oliver. Check all your organs are functioning properly, liver, kidneys, thyroid, that sort of thing. We may be looking at something as straightforward as iron deficiency, or possibly diabetes. I'd like a urine sample now, if you can manage that, and I'll have a feel of your tummy as you've mentioned abdominal pain and bowel changes. It could be any number of things, but I don't like to speculate, so I'd like to see you again in ten days please, and your lovely wife if she wants to come and that's okay with you. Let's put everyone's mind at rest."

Oliver had all the blood tests, and we returned to Doctor Simon's office at the appointed time. Doctor Simon was not able to put everyone's mind at rest. In fact, nothing could be further from the truth.

"I'll get straight to the point. I'm afraid it's not good news. From the blood results, and the fact you are somewhat jaundiced, although I cannot be one hundred percent certain, we are looking at the possibility that you have pancreatic cancer. I'm unable to tell you very much more at this point. You will need further, much more comprehensive testing, which I'm referring you for immediately. Please try not to worry, which of course you are bound to, which is understandable, but until we have a confirmed diagnosis, let's remain positive. I have spoken with my good friend Joe Sadiqqi, who is a top medical oncologist at the University Hospital, he will contact you with an appointment in the next couple of days. I'm so sorry I can't give you better news. Do you have any questions?"

I shook my head; tears had rendered me speechless. A voice that sounded like Oliver but not like Oliver, weak, timid and wobbly, asked the obvious question. "How long, Doctor? Will I live to see the twins?" I could see through my tears he was struggling to contain his own.

"Oliver, Hannah, let's take this one step at a time. We don't have a definitive diagnosis yet, and it would be wrong of me to give you any information that may be incorrect. You are a strong young man, and Joe Sadiqqi is an amazing oncologist. Let's see what he has to say before we go making assumptions, eh?"

We left his office in silence, which continued all the way home. I have very little recollection of the next few weeks, which comprised of many hospital visits, tests, more tests, and many tears. It was, as Doctor Simon had believed, pancreatic cancer, and quite advanced. We were looking at months, most likely, and neither of us were prepared to face it or even talk about it. At some point, we must have told our families, as they seemed to appear, as if by magic, when we needed some support. They also intuitively knew when we needed to be alone and stayed away. Oliver spent some time as an inpatient in the hospital, and I struggled with seeing him looking so weak, and un-Oliver like.

I was acutely aware of the pitying glances, imagining what the whisperers were saying. "Poor woman, pregnant and her husband is dying. I heard it was twins! Can you imagine?" I felt weak, pathetic and hopeless.

In a strange twist of fate, one of the nurses I didn't recognise from Oliver's ward approached me as I was leaving one day. "Hannah, isn't it? Hannah the shoe queen? I thought I recognised you. You probably don't remember me, Becca Bradley, from school, only I'm Becca Hope now. Is your husband the lovely Oliver? I've just been sent over from B2 for a stint on Oncology. How are you bearing up?"

"Oh, Becca, hello. Of course I remember you, the best Goal Attack the school netball team ever had. I'm… yes, Oliver is my husband and… I… He…" and the tears came again, this time with great big heaving sobs. Becca took my arm and led me to a small room at the end of the corridor, pushing the door shut behind her with her foot. She sat me down and knelt on the floor in front of the chair, wrapping her arms around me while I sobbed, quite an achievement with me being so heavily pregnant.

I have no idea how long we were there and, every time I tried to get myself together, she just said quietly, "Hannah, just let it out. You need to do this, and we'll stay here for as long as it takes."

Eventually the sobs subsided, and I took a deep breath. Before I could speak, Becca said, "Don't even think of saying you're sorry. That absolutely needed to happen. Stay right there, I'll get us some tea, I'll be right back."

True to her word, she was back in minutes, with two mugs of lukewarm tea. We sat in comfortable silence for a while, sipping the tea, then she said, "Don't look so worried, I have finished my shift today. I'd like to talk with you, but not at the hospital. How would you feel about meeting up for a coffee, no not a coffee, most pregnant women can't stomach it, but tea? No pressure, but I'd like to help you in any way I can. I'll give you my number and you can text, call or not call. Just know that you have another friend, okay?" I nodded, and thanked her, several times. She hugged me and, as I left, called softly after me, "Love the shoes, by the way. You were always a fashionista." I looked down at my feet and realised that, although my shoes were a similar style – flat and practical – one was brown and the other was blue. I laughed to myself and continued home, still smiling when I got there.

I sent Becca a text the next day and we arranged to meet up the following week. As Oliver was now out of hospital, a few of his work friends came over with pizzas and alcohol-free beer, so I left them to it for a couple of hours and met up with Becca. She came armed with leaflets, pamphlets and a tonne of phone numbers and websites that I might find helpful. We talked non-stop for two hours. In truth, after a few gently probing questions, I did most of the talking. Becca was a great listener and seemed to really understand my fears. I sensed there was more to her than I had first thought, that she was a woman I once went to school with, who was also a very kind nurse.

"How did you get to be so understanding? It's like you're in my head, knowing what I'm thinking almost before I know I'm thinking it. I find it so easy to talk to you about everything, particularly about Oliver. What is your superpower, I wonder?" I smiled.

"Four years ago, I was on duty in A&E, on the trauma team. There was a terrible accident on the ring road involving a truck, two cars and a motorbike," she began.

I nodded. "I remember that being on the television, it was terrible, wasn't it?"

"It was, and as the nearest hospital with a major trauma unit, the two cars' drivers and the biker were brought to our A&E department. It's a tough job for the team, but it's all hands on deck when there is a critical incident. I was working on the female driver of the first car, when I saw the rider of the motorbike. That was Mike, my husband, and despite the efforts of everyone, he didn't make it. So, I've had my own struggles, Hannah, and if anything good can come out of something so awful, it's made me forever grateful for what Mike and I had, and determined to help others in any way I can. The love and support I received from so many people, family, friends and even total strangers, carried me through the darkest moments of my life. And don't feel sorry for me, please, I'm doing as well as I can be, and I think Mike and I were so lucky to have had what many people never experience, a deep love that will last a lifetime. So, there we are. And you need to get back to your husband. How about meeting again on Tuesday?"

That was the beginning of a strong and lasting friendship with Becca.

Oliver and I muddled through the following weeks, both trying to help and support the other, often too exhausted to be able to do much. I kept telling myself that being pregnant with twins was nothing compared to what Oliver was going through, and I needed to up my game. Oliver was frustrated that he couldn't do as much physically as he wanted to and was struggling with feeling helpless. When the washing machine stopped working, he wanted to try to pull it out from under the worktop but didn't have the strength to and, even if I had the strength to, had no chance with my ever-expanding bump. It was the first time I saw him cry, and it was heartbreaking. His tears were not self-pity, just frustration that he couldn't help me. He said he felt awful that he was letting me down, he was unable to honour his promise to take care of me and so on. Trying to reassure him, we nearly ended up in a row; he was angry with himself, and I was angry with him for being angry with himself, as none of this was his fault. We were going round in circles with it when Louisa stopped by. Oblivious to the tension in the room, she asked why the washing machine was sticking out.

"Well, because it's broken and I'm such a weakling and Freddie is the size of a small village," Oliver retorted with an attempt at a grin.

In a few seconds, Louisa had the machine out and was asking for a screwdriver. Half an hour later, the machine was fixed and back in place. We were speechless.

"That's why you shouldn't judge a book by its cover," Louisa said, laughing. "I may only be five foot two, and seven stone ten pounds, but I'm a lean, mean, washing machine queen. That comes from living on my own and having limited funds. I can fix most things; do you have a toilet needing unblocking or a shed needing to be built?" Thank heavens for Louisa, we were all laughing now. And she helped to finish decorating the nursery and helped Oliver build the cots, bless her.

Friends and family got us through those weeks and months, while Oliver was in and out of hospital, and my bump seemed to grow to epic proportions. My midwife had arranged for a planned c-section for the twins, which I was disappointed about, but we had to think about the safest option for all of us. Amongst other things, my blood pressure was on the high side, so we did as advised by the experts. Oliver was back in hospital at the time, which was probably a plus, as they wheeled him down to the delivery room in a wheelchair and he had a nurse with him, so the team could focus on the delivery. The truth is, I hadn't given a great deal of thought to what would happen after the twins were born, so I was surprised to discover that both our mothers, my sister Grace, Michelle, Scott and Becca had set up a WhatsApp group and had everything under control. The births were quite straightforward and, on the 15th of December at eleven-twenty in the morning, we became the proud parents of Eva Marie and Olivia Rachel – in our opinion, the most beautiful babies to have ever been born – and all four of us were home in time for Christmas, the 24th of December to be precise.

Our wonderful support team had decorated the house, very simply but beautifully. The fridge and freezer were full, and there were gifts under the tree. We spent Christmas morning as the new little family of four we had become, in awe of our two beautiful daughters. Our Christmas dinner was delivered at one o'clock by Oliver's dad Jack, who said we would be having timed short visits from as many of the family as we could manage, spaced throughout the afternoon, if that would be okay with us. We agreed and promised him we would say if it was too much. In fact, it was lovely, as Oliver seemed to have rallied dramatically since the twins' arrival and had more energy than he had experienced in weeks. He had even managed to eat a small amount of his Christmas dinner. I did have to help him eat the pudding, but eating two portions of pudding is never a problem for me.

As promised, our visitors came in short bursts, starting with Michelle, Scott and the children. Ricky and Kent spoke in whispers, so as not to wake their new cousins, and they had each brought a toy car for the girls to play with. Their own idea, obviously. They stayed for around twenty minutes, and half an hour after they had left, Sylvia and Jack arrived. Oliver and Jack fed the girls, while Sylvia took me into the kitchen. She was struggling to hold back her tears.

"Hannah, I just want to say how happy we are that Oliver found you. We all know what is coming and want you to know how grateful we are to you. You have made our son so happy, and the twins are the icing on the cake. Jack and I see you as a daughter, and we always will. Thank you, for all you have done and are doing, and we will be here for you all." Her voice cracked, and we hugged in silence for a full minute, unable to hold back our tears.

"Any chance of a cup of tea in here, Freddie? Honestly, Dad, what is it with these modern wives? The service here is terrible, isn't it?" Oliver and Jack were laughing as Sylvia pretended to clip Oliver's ear. Jack went into the kitchen and made the tea.

Becca called round an hour after Jack and Sylvia left, with a pair of beautiful pink and white blankets for the girls. I told her how grateful I was that she had found time for us on Christmas Day.

"On the contrary, my friends. I'm grateful you gave me a chance to escape for half an hour today. Honestly, my kids have been squabbling since daybreak, my dad has been snoring in front of the telly all afternoon and my mum has checked the bin to see what was ready made and told me off for not making my own pigs in blankets, bread sauce or Christmas pudding. Honestly, they're unbelievable!" It was good to see Oliver laughing so much.

My mum and Grace came in the early evening, with a cold meat and salad platter. As usual, my mother came straight to the point. "We don't want to intrude on you all, but we have worked out a rota for the coming weeks.

I've printed it off for you both to have a look at, and make sure you're happy with it. As you'll see, we have Michelle on three mornings a week, while Sylvia and Jack take care of Cassidy, Grace on two mornings a week, which gives you the weekends to fend for yourselves. Becca is going to do the night shift on a Monday, I'll do Wednesday and Thursday nights, and we'll see how things work out. If you need more help, we'll cross that bridge, and if you need less, that's fine, too. No rush to make any decisions either way, talk it through together later. Now, where are you hiding those beautiful granddaughters of mine? Don't worry, I promise not to wake them but is it okay if I have a little peep? Oliver?"

Oliver, always in awe of the whirlwind that calls herself my mother, just nodded and pointed to the nursery. She tiptoed across the room, glancing back at Grace with her finger to her lips looking every bit the baddie in a pantomime. I gave Oliver my 'I'm sorry about my mother' look and he smiled and shrugged.

As things turned out, we did not require the level of help that had been suggested for quite some time. The twins were perfect in every way, they slept, we fed and changed them, they slept again. Oliver seemed to be almost on hold with the cancer; although there were regular hospital appointments and a lot of medication, he seemed stable, although he was losing weight at an alarming rate, and was very tired.

One morning, Jack appeared unannounced. He informed me that Sylvia and my mum would be over shortly to take me and the twins out for a couple of hours. Apparently, an appointment had been made at the hairdresser's for me, and we were booked in at Carmello's for lunch.

"Thought I could spend the morning with you, old chap, if that's okay? Give us both a break from all these women?" Now I knew where Oliver got his humour.

I was beginning to realise just how lucky we were, in so many ways. Obviously, Oliver's cancer was the worst thing imaginable, but our families were so thoughtful and supportive, we were truly lucky to have such wonderful people around us. I changed out of my tracksuit bottoms and was surprised to find I could fit into my jeans. Admittedly they were a little snug, but I got them on. I'd just have to be mindful of that at lunch. Heels were out of the question, especially with carrying the girls, so I settled on pink loafers and a floaty top. By the time the mothers arrived, Oliver and Jack had made up formula and packed enough nappies for two days, just in case.

I hadn't been to a hairdresser's in months, and it was just what I needed. The mums walked the twins' pushchair around the shops while I was pampered. It seemed my hair had grown horizontally during the pregnancy, so while the hairdresser didn't take much off the length, she spent a long time 'taking some of the weight out'. By the time the mothers returned, I was looking and feeling more like my old self. My mum had pre-paid and tipped for my hair, bless her, and Sylvia was in the chair for lunch. They had realised we were not as financially comfortable as we had been. Lunch was amazing. I had a fabulous prawn and asparagus pasta with sun-dried tomatoes and wilted spinach in a lobster sauce, feeling a teeny bit guilty that Oliver and Jack were probably having a cheese sandwich. On those grounds, I opted for tiramisu in a 'to-go box', a thing we had discovered in America. Tiramisu was Oliver's favourite. The twins woke just as we were contemplating coffee, which was a blessing, as I was back on it, thankfully, so we fed them while we chatted over cappuccino.

When we arrived home, Jack and Oliver were also sitting drinking coffee. Oliver whistled, "Wow, hello gorgeous lady. Looks like I have my beautiful Freddie back. I thought you may have been an impostor under all that hair. And you come bearing gifts, how lucky am I?" Under his brave exterior, I could tell he had been crying. I waited until everyone had gone and the girls were settled before asking him about it.

"Where do I start? Yes, I was emotional, Jack told me how proud he was of all of us and grateful to be my dad. He said Scott and I have been the best sons a man could ask for, and how devastated he and Mum are about my cancer. Since we first knew this was a death sentence, he and Mum have been racking their brains on how to help us. He said they have worked hard to leave us secure financially when they die, but as it looks like I'm going first, they have sold their place in South Africa. The upshot is, they want to pay off our mortgage and put a lump sum in the bank to tide us over – well, you over – until you're in a position to return to work at some point when the girls are older.

They have talked it through with Scott and Michelle, who are a hundred percent on board. They have also spoken with their solicitor about the tax implications and suchlike. Provided they both live for seven years, it should be fine. I tried to object, but Dad was insistent. He said it's his job to provide for you and the girls as I won't be able to. Freddie, it feels horrible and wrong, but I don't see that we have a choice. I need to know you'll be okay when I've gone. I feel I'm letting you down, I can't begin to tell you how sorry I am," and he started to cry again.

I reassured him that he wasn't letting me down at all, he'd given me the best years of my life, and two beautiful daughters. We both cried and held each other for a very long time, until the girls woke up. Together, we fed and bathed them and played with them. I watched Oliver taking it all in. He knew there wouldn't be many more opportunities for him to be a doting father, and it broke my heart.

It Takes One Shoe

In the following weeks, we had no choice but to put Mum's rota into practice. Oliver spoke about a hospice, but I wouldn't hear of it. He was my husband, and I was determined we, with the help and support of our families and friends, would be together however hard it got. Becca set up all kinds of help, and somehow we muddled through. We took thousands of photos, such as Oliver bathing or feeding the girls. There is one picture that, to this day, makes me cry. Oliver was lying in bed, with a twin tucked under each arm, struggling to stay awake. Both of the girls are looking up at him, studying his face intently, almost as if they are committing every detail of him to memory, like they somehow knew he wouldn't be around for long.

One morning soon after that picture was taken, Mum and Michelle were taking care of the twins, and I was lying on the bed next to Oliver. He had been in bed for three days, and he showed no sign of being able or willing to get up, other than to use the bathroom.

"Freddie, listen carefully, could you?" His voice was quiet, barely above a whisper. He spoke slowly, pausing often to catch his breath. "There are letters in my desk for you and the girls and my parents, along with some other stuff, including funeral wishes. I'm so sorry you must do this. But I want to tell you something, too. I want you to know how much I love you. Since you first face-planted the pavement and threw your chow mein at me, I loved you. Your crazy shoe obsession, even your Minnie Mouse slippers, your wild hair, your manic laughter, I love everything about you. Our trip to Italy was the most fun I ever had, our wedding, our honeymoon in Florida, our incredible daughters, so many wonderful memories. I'm grateful to you for every single day we've had together, and for making me happier than any man has a right to be. If I could live another fifty years in exchange for not having you in my life, I wouldn't take it. Please be happy, Freddie, I know it'll be hard for you, but you must get on with your life and be a happy mum to Eva and Olivia. And I hope I will always be with you, watching over you all from another place. I will love you forever, Freddie." And his eyes closed.

For three long days and nights we watched him sleeping. His parents stayed along with my mum, all sleeping in chairs or on the lounge floor. Scott and Michelle came and said goodbye to Oliver, as did many friends. Becca slipped in and out, as did the nurses who cleaned him and monitored and adjusted his medication through a syringe. On the morning of the fourth day, Oliver's breathing changed. Becca nodded to me. "Would you like to bring the girls in? And Sylvia and Jack?" I nodded and went to wake Oliver's parents. I took the sleeping twins in and laid them beside Oliver. Jack and Sylvia sat on one side of the bed, and I laid on the other.

"Do you want to be on your own?" asked Sylvia. I shook my head.

"He's not just my Oliver, he's special to us all," I whispered. Leaning in close, I stroked his head and kissed his cheek. "Goodnight, my darling, thank you for being the most incredible husband and father. We love you so much. Sleep peacefully, my love." As my tears fell onto his face, Oliver took his last breath.

I have no idea how long I laid there beside him, or who took the twins back to their bedroom. In fact, I have no memory of the next three days. The only thing that brought me back to reality was Becca saying, "We have two little babies here who have lost their dad. However shit you are feeling, and I know you're in a big black hole right now, these girls need their mummy and you're all they have, so let's get you in the shower while I make you something to eat." Almost on autopilot, I did as I was told. For days, I was like a robot, planning my husband's funeral with his parents, notifying the relevant authorities, feeling completely numb.

It was the twins that brought me out of the padded cell my mind was in. They both became ill within twenty-four hours of each other. It was only really a heavy cold, but I was paranoid it may be something more. Again, Becca came to the rescue.

"It's a cold, Hannah, nothing more. They will be fine, but I understand what you're thinking. You have just lost

Oliver, and you're terrified something might happen to them. You need to take a breath and remember how many people are on your team. We are all here, nothing else bad is going to happen, we'll make sure of it."

Of course she was right, and it made me think about losing a child. What on earth must Sylvia and Jack be feeling right now? I couldn't begin to imagine, but I did realise how selfish I was being, relying on everyone else to take care of my children while trying to deal with their own grief. Asking Becca to take care of the girls for an hour, I explained I needed to go to see Sylvia and Jack and why. She just smiled and said, "Welcome back, Hannah."

I spent an hour with Oliver's parents, apologising for being so selfish and not recognising their pain. They, of course, were gracious and wonderful. We all cried but we also laughed for the first time. "Can you believe Oliver has insisted we all wear pink to the funeral? And the music choices? We'll have to tell everyone it's Oliver's choices and nothing to do with us. He's certainly having the last laugh up there."

The day of the funeral, the weather couldn't make up its mind. First sunshine, then clouds, then drizzle, then another glimpse of the sun. Everyone was ready, including the twins, half an hour before the cars were due to arrive. Scott passed round brandy for all the adults. They had arranged for Mrs Mac, the neighbour, to have Cassidy and the boys were at school. We had all agreed the girls should be there; although still small babies, Oliver was their dad, and it was the right thing to do. They would be glad when they were older, I hoped.

As the funeral cortege arrived, I checked my bag for the poem I was planning to read at the service and slipped on my 'Oliver shoes', my favourite sage green shoes with the gold trim. I figured it would work, as my pink floral dress had green leaves in the pattern. When I saw Oliver's coffin, I started to shake uncontrollably. My mum took my arm to walk outside, and I swear I heard Oliver's voice, "You've got this, Freddie; I'm right beside you."

The journey to the crematorium seemed a long way, but I was wishing it was even longer as the thought of the final goodbye was overwhelming. Jack and Sylvia sat one either side of me, holding my hands, with Scott and Michelle behind us in the limousine. My mum and Grace took the girls with Becca. When we pulled into the crematorium, the crowd of people waiting took my breath away; so many people wanted to say goodbye, it lifted my heart. After the congregation was seated, the five of us followed Oliver's coffin in, to the strains of 'I've Had the Time of My Life' by Bill Medley and Jennifer Warnes.

There were tributes read by Scott and Jack, the eulogy read by the celebrant and then more music; of course, it was Queen's 'Don't Stop Me Now', which made us all laugh through our tears. Then it was my turn to read the poem I had written. With legs like jelly, I walked to the front and took a deep breath.

"Oliver wanted today to be a celebration of his life, of fun memories and things that make us smile, so I've written something to honour him.

I always thought men are like shoes, we never know which ones to choose.

Some are too high, others too tight, and rarely we find the ones just right.

But then I found the perfect pair, I just looked up and you were there.

So comfortable, a perfect fit, somehow, we knew that this was it.

My perfect man, so kind and fun, I always knew you were the one.

You gave so much, enriched my life, I feel so blessed to be your wife.

And now you're gone, eternal sleep, but in my heart, I'll always keep

My memories, the love we share, I know that you're forever there.

Cinderella said, 'It takes one shoe', and Oliver, that shoe was you."

We walked out into the bright sunshine to another Queen song, 'Another One Bites the Dust' and Oliver had his final wish: everyone smiling.

Epilogue

Watching Eva and Olivia being chased along the shore by their cousins, Kent, Ricky and Cassidy, all laughing trying to tag one another, makes me smile. I feel warm, not just from the Florida sun, but warm deep inside, a kind of inner peace. The first three years after Oliver died were the hardest times of my life, trying to raise the girls alone, finding myself back in the workplace, feeling like I was constantly spinning plates in the air. If it wasn't for the unwavering support of our families, I'm not sure I would have survived, but survive I did, and finally I have come to a place of acceptance, even peace.

Today we all are here to celebrate Oliver's birthday with a champagne toast and cake on the beach. Yes, that was a crazy idea, but we are a crazy family. In the years that have passed, the girls have grown into beautiful young ladies, albeit with wild hair like me. They look identical, but they have very different personalities. Olivia is so like Oliver: thoughtful, kind and always ready to see the best in people, with the patience of a saint. Eva, bless her, is prone to clumsiness, disasters follow wherever she goes, but she has a wonderful sense of humour and is happy to be the butt of any joke. Strangely, they both love shoes. We are thriving, and although we will always miss Oliver, we are happy. I have realised that I may never need any more shoes, I'm most comfortable in my bare feet anyway. As I watch the girls getting ice cream with their grandparents, I'm smiling. Whenever I have a little wobble, I can hear Oliver as though he's here: "You've got this, Freddie; I'm right beside you."

Acknowledgements

There are so many people who have had a supporting role in this story and I'm immensely grateful to them all.

Firstly, a super-sized thank you to Jen Parker of Fuzzy Flamingo, without whose expert knowledge, advice, support, hard work and encouragement every step of the way, the book would still be on my laptop, unread. Jen gave me the confidence to believe I could do it, and when someone with Jen's experience believes in you, anything is possible.

Callum from Solent computers in Lee-on-Solent, who fully understood my technophobia. He assured me I was not an idiot and put all my random documents and files into some semblance of order to be able to send to Jen as a proper manuscript. Thank you.

Thank you to the un-named people, who may recognise some of themselves in the characters included in the book. I apologise but thank you for giving me inspiration.

My wonderful niece Carole, who is like a daughter to me, my guinea pig reader with the first draft. She always has my back but is never afraid to be brutally honest. Thank you.

My good friend Shelley, who took my tantrums in her stride with a smile and a hug, thank you.

My dear friends, Terri, Becky, Lou, Debbie, Karen, Jane, Michele, Erin, Maxine, Sophie, Anne, and my long-suffering sister who all believed in me when I felt like someone had turned off the light at the end of the tunnel. I'm sorry if I made your ears bleed at times. My heartfelt thanks to each of you. Even my lovely dentist Sarah and her team were all supportive and encouraging, thank you all.

Anna, the hairdresser who started the ball rolling by laughing at my anecdotes and telling me I should write a book, bless you. This is all your fault.

My wonderful friend and late mother-in-law, D, the original shoe queen. Thank you for always believing in me, I'm hoping you can get a copy up there, I miss you.

My long-suffering husband, who can finally accept it was not just another one of my harebrained schemes, I finally did it; thank you for standing by me when I may have been a teeny-weeny bit grouchy on occasion.

And finally, you, the reader, thank you so much for taking the time out to read it, I hope you enjoyed reading it as much as I loved writing it. Please do leave a review on Amazon, as it really helps other readers to find my book.